ᐅᓂᒃᑲᖅᑎᒌᑦ

ᐅᑭᐅᖅᑕᖅᑑᒥ ᓯᓚᐅᑉ ᖃᓄᐃᓐᓇᓕᓂᒃ
ᐅᓂᒃᑲᓕᔭᐅᑦ ᓄᓇᕗᒻᒥ ᓱᕈᓯᕐᓇᓄᑦ

UNIKKAAQATIGIIT

Arctic Weather and Climate Through
the Eyes of Nunavut's Children

Edited by   David Natcher

Mary Ellen Thomas

Neil Christopher

Published by Inhabit Media Inc.
www.inhabitmedia.com

Inhabit Media Inc. (Iqaluit), P.O. Box 11125, Iqaluit, Nunavut, X0A 1H0
(Toronto), 146A Orchard View Blvd., Toronto, Ontario, M4R 1C3

Editors: David Natcher, Mary Ellen Thomas, and Neil Christopher
Translator: Rachel A. Qitsualik-Tinsley
Photographers: Tim Kalusha, Shelley Ross, B&C Alexander/Arcticphoto, and Arctic Kingdom
Art Director: Ellen Ziegler

We acknowledge the support of the Canada Council for the Arts for our publishing program.

Printed in Canada.

Library and Archives Canada Cataloguing in Publication

    Unikkaatiqatigiit : ukiuqtaqtumi silanga ammalu silaup qanuinninga
Inuit surusit qanuq tukisinirijanginnik unikkaat = Unikkaaqatigiit : arctic
weather and climate through the eyes of Inuit children / edited by David
Natcher, Mary Ellen Thomas, Neil Christopher.

Title in Inuktitut syllabics romanized.
Translated from the Inuktitut and English by Rachel A. Qitsualik.
Text in Inuktitut and English.
ISBN 978-1-927095-49-2

    1. Arctic regions--Climate--Literary collections. 2. Children--Arctic regions--
Literary collections. 3. Inuit--Canada--Literary collections. 4. Arctic regions--
Literary collections. 5. Inuit literature--Canada. 6. Canadian literature (English)--
Inuit authors. I. Natcher, David C., 1967- II. Christopher, Neil, 1972-
III. Thomas, Mary Ellen, 1951- IV. Title: Arctic weather and climate through
the eyes of Inuit children. V. Title: Unikkaaqatigiit : arctic weather and climate
through the eyes of Inuit children.

PS8235.C4U55 2013   C897'.1208036   C2013-902205-8

UNIVERSITY OF
SASKATCHEWAN

Nunavut

ᓄᓇᕗᑦ ᓯᓚᑦᑐᖅᓴᕐᕕᒃ
Nunavut
Arctic College

Canada Council
for the Arts

Conseil des Arts
du Canada

Canada

Canadian
Heritage
Patrimoine
canadien

ᐅᓂᒃᑲᖅᑲᑎᒌᑦ

ᐅᑭᐅᖅᑲᑕᖅᑑᒥ ᓯᓚᐅᑉ ᖃᓄᐃᖕᓂᖓᓂᒃ
ᐅᓂᒃᑲᓕᖅᔭᐅᑎᒡ ᓄᓇᕗᒻᒥ ᓯᐳᓯᖕᒋᕐᓂᐊᓄᑦ

UNIKKAAQATIGIIT

Arctic Weather and Climate Through
the Eyes of Nunavut's Children

Edited by David Natcher
Mary Ellen Thomas
Neil Christopher

ᓯᑎᑦᑐᑦ ᐅᖃᖅᑐᔪᑦ...07

ᐅᓂᒃᑲᖅᑐᐊᑦ ᐊᔾᔨᙳᐊᑦᓗ ᓄᓇᓕᐅᓂᖕ
ᐊᑐᖅᑕᐅᑦᓘᓂ

    ᐊᖅᐱᐊᑦ..11

    ᑎᕆᒐᕐᔪᐊᖅ 15

    ᑲᖕᖏᖅᑐᓂᖅ 25

    ᕿᖕᒥᐃᑦ...31

    ᐃᖅᑐᐃᑦ 35

    ᐸᖕᓂᖅᑐ 43

    ᓇᓂᓯᐱᒃ 49

    ᒥᑎᒪᑕᓕᒃ...53

    ᐃᒃᐱᐊᕐᔪᒃ 59

    ᖅᐅᕐᓯᐃᑐᖅ 65

    ᐊᐅᕐᓯᐃᑐᖅ 69

Foreword 09

Stories and Pictures

    Arviat 11

    Whale Cove 15

    Rankin Inlet 25

    Cape Dorset 31

    Iqaluit 35

    Pangnirtung 43

    Nanisivik 49

    Pond Inlet 53

    Arctic Bay 59

    Resolute Bay 65

    Grise Fiord 69

ᓯᕗᓪᓖᑦ ᐅᖃᐅᓰᑦ

ᑖᓐᓇ ᑲᑎᖅᓱᖅᓯᒪᔪᓂᒃ ᐅᓂᒃᑳᓕᖕᓂᑦ ᑲᑎᙵᔪᓂᒃ ᐅᖃᓕᒫᒐᒃᓴᓕᐊᖑᔪᖅ ᓯᕗᓪᓖᑦᑐᒥᒃ ᑎᑎᕋᖅᓯᒪᔪᓂᒃ ᓇᐃᑦᑐᓂᓗ ᑎᑎᕋᐅᔭᕐᓂᑯᓂᒃ ᒪᒃᑯᒃᑐᓄᑦ ᐃᓕᓐᓂᐊᖅᑎᓄᑦ ᑲᓇᑕᐅᑉ ᐅᑭᐅᖅᑕᖅᑐᖓᓂᒥᐅᓄᑦ ᐃᓚᒋᔭᐅᓪᓗᓂ ᐅᑭᐅᖅᑕᖅᑐᒥ ᓯᓚᐅᑉ ᖃᓄᐃᓐᓂᖓᓂᒃ ᑲᒪᔨᖏᓐᓄᑦ ᓵᓚᒃᓴᐅᑎᓕᕆᓂᐅᓪᓗᓂ. ᓯᕗᓕᐅᖅᑎᐅᑎᓪᓗᒋᑦ ᐊᕙᑎᓕᕆᔨᒃᑯᑦ ᑲᓇᑕᒥ ᐊᕐᕌᒍᑕᒫᑦ ᐱᒋᐊᖅᓱᑎᒃ 1994ᒥᑦ 1998ᒧᑦ, ᓵᓚᒃᓴᐅᑎᓕᕆᓂᖅ ᐃᑲᔪᕈᑕᐅᓯᒪᔪᖅ ᓱᕈᓯᕐᓄᑦ ᐃᓕᓐᓂᐊᕈᑕᐅᓪᓗᓂ ᓇᖕᒥᓂᖅ ᓇᔪᖅᑕᒥᓂ ᖃᓄᖅ ᓯᓚᖓᑦ ᖃᓄᐃᓐᓂᖓᓂᒃ ᖃᐅᔨᒪᔭᓐᓇᕐᒪᖔᕐᒥᒃ. ᐊᔾᔨᒌᙱᑦᑐᑦ ᐱᓕᕆᐊᒃᓴᑦ ᑕᒪᒃᑯᓇᙵᑦ ᑎᑎᕋᖅᑕᐅᓯᒪᔪᓂᑦ ᐊᒻᒪᓗ ᑎᑎᖅᑐᒐᕐᓂ ᑦ ᐱᔾᔪᑎᖃᖅᑐᑦ ᐅᓪᓗᑕᒫᑦ ᐊᒃᑐᐃᓂᕆᖃᑦᑕᖅᑕᖓᓂᑦ ᓯᓚᐅᑉ ᖃᓄᐃᓐᓂᖓᓂᒃ ᓄᓇᓕᖕᓂ ᐊᒻᒪᓗ ᐊᔾᔨᒌᙱᑦᑐᓄᑦ. ᒪᑯᐊ ᓄᓇᓕᖕᓂᒥᐅᓄᑦ ᑐᕌᖓᒧᑦ ᐅᓂᒃᑳᖅᑐᐊᒐᓚᐃᓪᓗ, ᖃᐅᔨᒪᓂᑐᖃᐃᓪᓗ, ᓯᓚᐅᑉ ᐊᓯᔾᔨᖅᐸᓪᓕᐊᓂᖓᑦ, ᐊᒻᒪᓗ ᐱᒻᒪᕆᐅᓂᖓᑦ ᐊᑦᑕᕐᓇᖅᑕᐃᓕᓂᐅᑉ ᒥᒃᓵᓄᑦ.

ᓄᓇᓕᖕᒥᐅᑦ ᐃᓐᓇᑐᖃᐃᑦ, ᐃᓅᓯᓕᒫᕐᒥᖕᓂ ᑲᒪᒋᔭᑐᖃᐅᔪᑦ ᐅᑭᐅᖅᑕᖅᑐᑉ ᓯᓚᖓᓂᒃ, ᓄᑕᕋᐅᓂᕐᒥᓂᒃ ᐱᒋᐊᖅᓱᑎᒃ, ᐅᓪᓚᕋᖅᑕᓚᐅᖅᑐᑦ ᐃᓕᓐᓂᐊᕐᕕᓐᓄᐊᖅᑎᑕᐅᓪᓗᑎᒃ ᖃᐅᔨᒪᔭᕐᒥᖕᓂᒃ ᐃᓕᓐᓂᐊᖅᑎᑦᑎᓪᓗᓂᒃ ᐊᑐᖅᓯᒪᔭᕐᒥᖕᓂᓪᓗ ᐅᓂᒃᑲᐅᓯᖃᖅᓱᑎᒃ. ᐃᓐᓇᑐᖃᐃᑦ ᐅᔾᔨᕆᒋᐊᖃᕐᓂᕐᒥᒃ ᓯᓚᒥᒃ ᖃᐅᔨᒃᑲᐃᓚᐅᖅᑐᑦ ᓯᓚᒥᒃ ᖃᓄᐃᓐᓂᖓᓂᒃ ᒪᓕᒋᐊᖃᕐᓂᕐᒥᒃ—ᖃᓄᕐᓗ ᐊᓄᕆ ᒪᓕᖕᓂᖃᕐᒪᖔᑦ ᓄᕗᔭᐅᑉ ᑕᖅᓴᖓᑕ ᑕᐅᑦᑐᖓᓂᒃ, ᓯᓚᐅᓪᓗ ᐃᓕᖅᑯᓯᕆᓂᐊᖅᑕᖓᓂᒃ ᖃᐅᔨᒪᓂᕐᒥᒃ ᑲᓪᓗᖕᓂᐊᕐᓂᖓᓂᒃ, ᑕᒃᓯᖃᕐᓂᐊᕐᓂᖓᓂᒃ, ᓇᓗᓇᐃᖅᓯᓪᓗᓂ ᐊᓄᕆᑐᓂᐊᕐᓂᖓᓂᒃ.

ᐱᕙᓪᓕᐊᑎᑕᐅᔪᖅ ᐱᖓᓱᓂᒃ ᑐᕌᕈᑎᖃᓚᐅᖅᑐᖅ. ᓯᕗᓪᓕᖅᐸᐅᔪᖅ ᐸᐸᑕᐅᓂᖓᑦ ᐅᓂᒃᑳᖅᑐᐊᑐᖃᐃᑦ ᐊᒻᒪᓗ ᐃᓕᖅᑯᓯᑐᖃᐃᑦ ᐅᑭᐅᖅᑕᖅᑐᒥ ᓯᓚᖓᓂᒃ ᐱᔾᔪᑎᓖᑦ—ᐃᓐᓇᑐᖃᓄᑦ ᐅᓂᒃᑲᐅᓯᒃᑯᑦ ᑲᔪᓯᑎᑕᐅᖃᑦᑕᖅᓯᒪᔪᑦ —ᐊᓯᐅᑎᑕᐅᖁᓇᒋᑦ. ᑐᓪᓕᐊ ᑐᕌᖅᑕᐅᔪᖅ ᒪᒃᑯᒃᑐᐃᑦ ᐅᔾᔨᓂᖅᕈᓐᓇᕐᓴᖅᐸᑕ ᐃᓐᓇᑐᖃᐃᑦ ᓯᓚᑐᓂᖏᓐᓂᒃ ᐃᓕᖅᑯᓯᑐᖃᑐᐃᓐᓇᕐᓄᑦ ᑭᓯᐊᓂ ᑐᕌᖓᙱᑦᑐᑎᒃ. ᑭᓯᐊᓂᑦᑕᐅᖅ ᓯᓚᓗᒃᑐᒥ ᐱᔪᓐᓇᕐᓂᕐᒥᑦ ᐃᓕᑕᐅᖁᓪᓗᒋᑦ ᓯᕗᒻᒧᓪᓗ ᐊᓐᓇᒍ ᓇᕈᑕᐅᓗᑎᒃ, ᐱᓗᐊᖅᑐᒥᒃ ᐅᑭᐅᖅᑕᖅᑐᑉ ᐊᔾᔨᒋᔭᐅᙱᑦᑐᑉ ᓯᓚᖓ ᐱᓪᓗᒍ. ᑭᖑᓪᓕᖅᐹᖅ ᑐᕌᖅᑕᐅᔪᖅ ᓵᓚᒃᓴᖅᓯᐊᕐᓂᐅᓚᐅᖅᑐᖅ ᐃᓕᓐᓂᐊᖅᑎᓂᒃ ᐃᓯᒪᓕᓐᓕᐊᓕᖅᑎᑦᑎᓚᐅᖅᑐᖅ ᐃᓅᓯᖏᑕ ᒥᒃᓵᓄᑦ ᐊᒃᑐᖅᑕᐅᓂᖓᑦ ᓯᓚᐅᑉ ᐊᓯᔾᔨᖅᐸᓪᓕᐊᓂᖓᓂᑦ ᐱᔪᓂᑦ ᐅᑭᐅᖅᑕᖅᑐᒥ.

ᐅᓪᓗᒥᐅᔪᖅ, ᓯᓚᐅᑉ ᐊᓯᔾᔨᖅᐸᓪᓕᐊᓂᖓ ᐊᒃᓱᕈᕈᑕᐅᖕᒪᑦ ᓯᓚᕐᔪᐊᑦᑎᓐᓂ, ᐊᒻᒪᓗ ᐱᓗᐊᖅᑐᒥ ᐅᑭᐅᖅᑕᖅᑐᒥ. ᑕᒫᓂᓗ ᐊᓯᔾᔨᕈᑕᐅᓪᓚᕆᒍᑎᐅᓪᓗᓂ ᓯᓚᐅᑉ ᐊᓯᔾᔨᖅᐸᓪᓕᐊᓂᖓ. ᑕᒪᒃᑯᓇᓂ ᑎᑎᕋᖅᑕᐅᓯᒪᔪᓂ ᑲᑎᖅᓱᖅᑕᐅᓯᒪᔪᓂ, ᓂᕆᐅᒋᔭᖅᑐᒍᑦ ᖃᓄᐃᓐᓂᖓ ᐃᓅᓯᕗᑦ ᐅᓂᒃᑳᕆᔭᐅᒐᔭᕐᓂᕐᒪᖓᓂᒃ, ᐊᒻᒪᓗ ᓯᕗᓂᕐᒧᑦ ᐸᕐᓇᐅᑎᒋᓯᒪᒍᓐᓇᕆᔭᐅᓪᓗᓂ. ᑖᒃᑯᐊ ᓴᓇᔭᐅᓯᒪᔪᑦ ᑎᑎᕋᖅᑕᐅᓯᒪᔪᑦ ᑕᐃᒪᓐᓇᑦᑎᐊᖅᑐᑦ ᑎᑎᕋᖅᑕᐅᓚᐅᕐᓂᖏᑎᑐᑦ ᑕᑯᒃᓴᐅᔪᑦ ᐋᖅᑭᒃᑕᐅᓯᒪᓂᖏᑦ ᒪᓕᒃᑕᐅᓪᓗᑎᒃ 1994-ᒥ. ᐃᓚᐅᓚᐅᖅᑐᑦ ᐃᓄᐃᑦ ᑎᑎᕋᓚᐅᖅᑐᑦ ᑎᑎᖅᑐᒐᓚᐅᖅᑐᓪᓗ ᐃᓅᔪᓐᓃᖅᓯᒪᔪᐃᓐᓇᕆᐊᓖᑦ, ᑭᓯᐊᓂᓕ ᐊᒃᓱᕈᓚᐅᕐᓂᖏᑦ ᑕᑯᒃᓴᐅᔭᓐᓇᖅᑐᑦ ᑭᖑᓂᖏᑎᒍᑦ.

ᐅᓂᒃᑳᖅᑐᐊᑦ ᐊᒻᒪᓗ ᓇᐃᑦᑐᑦ ᑭᐳᒃᑎᑕᐅᓯᒪᔪᑦ ᐅᖃᐅᓯᑐᖃᒥᓂᐅᔪᓂᑦ ᑎᑎᕋᖅᓯᒪᓚᖓᔪᑦ ᑕᖅᓴᖃᖅᑐᒥᒃ ᑲᓚᖕᒥᒃ ᑐᓄᖅᑎᑕᐅᓗᑎᒃ.

GRISE FIORD

RESOLUTE BAY

ARCTIC BAY ● NANISIVIK

● POND INLET

● PANGNIRTUNG

● CAPE DORSET

● IQALUIT

● RANKIN INLET

● WHALE COVE

● ARVIAT

Foreword

This anthology brings together for the first time writing, poetry, and illustrations created by young students across northern Canada as part of an Arctic Weather Centre contest. Hosted by Environment Canada annually from 1994 to 1998, the contest encouraged children to think and actively learn about their unique northern climate. The diverse issues raised by these writings and illustrations range from the day-to-day effects of weather on the lives of people in the community to legends and mythology, traditional knowledge, climate change, and the importance of safety.

Community elders, whose lives have depended on their knowledge of the most minute details of the Arctic skies since they, too, were children, visited classrooms to share their insight and experience. Elders revealed to students the importance of attuning oneself to the guidance of the sky—what colours and cloud formations indicate thunderstorms, blizzards, fog, or heavy wind.

The project had three main aims. The first was to prevent the traditional stories and mythology surrounding Arctic weather—often passed down orally by elders—from disappearing. The second was to encourage young people to recognize the wisdom of elders not only as a stronghold of culture, but as a tool for surviving the extreme weather patterns of the northern environment. Finally, the contest motivated students to think about how climate change impacts their lives and their Arctic environment.

Today, climate change continues to be of critical importance to our world, and in particular to the North, where its effects are felt most acutely. With the publication of this anthology, we hope to document a historical moment, while at the same time looking to the future. This work is presented exactly as it was written and drawn in 1994. Some of the people involved with the making of these pieces may have passed on, but their creativity is preserved here for posterity.

Stories and poems in the original language will be written against a coloured background.

ᐊᕐᕕᐊᑦ	Arviat
ᑎᑭᕋᕐᔪᐊᖅ	Whale Cove
ᑲᖏᖅᖠᓂᖅ	Rankin Inlet
ᑭᙵᐃᑦ	Cape Dorset
ᐃᖅᑲᓗᐃᑦ	Iqaluit
ᐸᖕᓂᖅᑑ	Pangnirtung
ᓇᓂᓯᕕᒃ	Nanisivik
ᒥᑦᑎᒪᑕᓕᒃ	Pond Inlet
ᐃᒃᐱᐊᕐᔪᒃ	Arctic Bay
ᖃᐅᓱᐃᑦᑐᖅ	Resolute Bay
ᐊᐅᔪᐃᑦᑐᖅ	Grise Fiord

ᐊᕐᕕᐊᑦ
ᕿᑎᖅᖂᖅ
ᐃᓕᓐᓂᐊᕐᕕᖠᔾᔪᐊᖅ

ᐊᕐᕕᐊᑦ ᕼᐋᒪᓚ°ᖠ ᓂᒋᖅᖂᑦᓯᐅᓂᖅᖅᑕᕐᔪᖅ ᓄᓇᖢᒥ ᓄᓇ°ᒥᖠᓂ, ᐊᒻᒪᓗ ᐃᓄᖅᑕᖢᓂ ᖅᑲᓂᕿᖠᓂᕐ 3,000. ᐊᕐᕕᐊᑦ ᕿᑲᒡᓗᖠᖅᓱᖅᓲᑦ, ᑑᒍᒡᑲᐅᖅᖢᒍᓗ, ᐊᒻᒪᓗ ᓄᓂᖅᓄᑦ ᐅᑉᑲᖅᑕᕐᕿᖕᑦᖢᓂ ᑕᓐᑐᔾᔪᑦ ᐊᖕᖅᕋᑎᓂᖢᓐᕐᑦ. ᐊᕐᕕᐊᕐᒥᑦᐅᑕᐃᑦᓗ ᖅᑲᐅᒪᓴᔭᐅᔭᑦ ᓴᓇᖕᖢᐊᖅᑎᐅᓂ°ᕋᐃᓄᑦ ᐅᔭᖅᖅᓂᖅ ᓴᓇᐅᓯᖕᕿᖅ. ᐅᔭᖅᖅᑎᑦ ᖕᐱᑎᖢᔾᐊᒐᒪᓄᑦ. ᐊᕐᕕᐊᑦ ᓄᓇ°ᖢ ᐊᖠᖢᑦ ᓚᖕᕿᐊᕐᔪᖅ, ᓄᓇᖅᖁᖅᑐᑦᖢᓂᖢ, ᐊᒡᒋᓂᖢᓗ ᑕᖢᖅᑲᖅᖢᓗᖢᓄ, ᑰᖕᕿᑦ ᐊᒡᕿᖢᑲᑕᑦᖢᓐᖤ, ᐊᒻᒪᓗ ᑐᐊᐸᖕᖤᖢᖤ ᐅᖅᖠᑐᖅᑲᐅᖅᖅᖢᓂᖢ. ᐊᕐᕕᐊᑦ ᓂᒋᖅᖂᑦᓯᐅᓂ°ᖢ ᐱᖠᒍᖢ, ᐊᐅᔭᒥ ᐃᓗ°ᖠᖢᑎᒥ ᐅᖅᖤᖕᔾᖁᑐᖕᖤᖢᑐᖅ 15°C-ᒥᑦ 20°C-ᒍᑦ. ᐅᑭᐅᒥ ᐃᖕᖠᖅᖅᑎᖢᑦᖣᑐ ᐁᖢᖤᐊᖠᑦ ᐊᒻᒪᓗ ᒫᖣᖖᑦᖤᖣᔾ, ᐱᖅᖠᔾᖕᖤᖅ ᐊᒻᒪᓗ ᐃᖠᖤᖠᓂ°ᖢ, ᐱᖢᐊᖅᑐᒦ ᐊᖂᑎᖣᑦᖢᖤᖢ, ᐃᖅᐱᖠ°ᖁᐭᖅᖤᑐᖅ -50°C-ᑎᑦᖤ.

The hamlet of Arviat is the southernmost mainland community of Nunavut, and has a population of almost 3,000. Arviat is home to polar bears, pods of beluga whales, and herds of migrating caribou. It is also known for the sculptures and carvings made by Arviarmiut, which use a robust local stone. Arviat's landscape is extremely flat, featuring long expanses of tundra, with small lakes, series of rivers, and gravel ridges. Because Arviat is so far south, in the summer it has average temperatures of 15°C to 20°C. In the cold winter months of February and March, blizzards occur and the temperature, with the wind chill, can feel like –50°C.

HOW FOG STARTED

A long time ago people say there was a man out on the land. He was followed by a polar bear and the man was trying to run away from the bear.

When the man swam across the river the polar bear asked him, "How did you pass the river?"

The man said, "I drank it and went across it."

Then the polar bear drank, and drank and when his stomach was too full he blew up. That's how fog started.

by: Annie Kaayak

ᖃᓄᖅ ᑕᒃᔭᖅ
ᐱᒋᐊᕐᑕᐅᕐᒪᖔᕆᑦ

ᐊᓂ ᑲᔭᒃ, ᒍᕆᑦ 8, ᐅᑭᐅᓖᑦ 13

ᑕᐊᒡᓕᓂᔪᖃᖅ ᐃᓄᐃᑦ ᐅᖃᐅᑎᖅᓯᒪᔭᖓᑦ ᐊᖕᖑᑎᒃᖅ ᓄᓇᒥ ᐊᖕᖓᓯᑎᖅᓯᒪᔭᖓᖅ. ᒪᓛᑕᐅᓂᖓᕐ ᓇᓄᕐᔪᑦ ᐊᒡᓗ ᓇᓄᖅ ᖃᒪᔾᔪᐊᔾᑎᖅᖃᓛᓂᕐᒧ. ᐊᖕᔪᑦ ᓇᓄᖕᑯᒥ ᐃᑲᖅᑐᖅ ᒍᒧᕐᖅ ᐊᒡᓗ ᓇᖕᖓᑕᑦ ᐊᐱᕆᓯᖅᑕᖃᓂᖕᖑᒃ, "ᖃᓄᕐᑦ ᒍᖕ ᑕᓚᖓ ᐃᑲᖅᐱᐱᕐᖅ?"

ᕿᐅᕐᐅᑦᓄᖓᕐ ᐊᖕᔪᖕᔪᑦ, "ᐃᒥᖅᔪ ᐃᑲᖅᑕ."

ᓇᖕᖓᑦ ᒍᖕ ᐃᒥᕐᖅᑕᑲᖕᖑᒃ, ᐊᒡᓗ ᐃᒥᕐᐊᖅᓂᕐᐅᒻᒪᖕᖑ ᓇᖕᖑᒃ ᖃᖕᖅᑐᐊᖕᖑᒃ. ᑕᐊᒪᖓᓇ ᐱᕐᑕᐅᕐᖅᑎᖕᑐᒍ ᐅᕐᑐᒥ ᑕᒃᔭᖕᖃᑦᖅᐱᑐᑦ.

How Fog Started
Annie Kaayak, Grade 8, Age 13

A long time ago people say there was a man out on the land. He was followed by a polar bear and the man was trying to run away from the polar bear.

When the man swam across the river the polar bear asked him, "How did you pass?"

The man said, "I drank it and went across it."

Then the polar bear drank and drank, and when his stomach was too full he blew up.

That is how the fog started.

ᐅᓂᒃᑳᖅ ᐱᔾᔪᑎᓕᒃ ᑲᓇᖕᓇᒥᒃ ᐊᒻᒪᓗ ᐱᖕᒐᖕᓇᒥᒃ

ᑯᑭᒃ ᑕᕐᒐᓕᒃ

ᐃᓐᓇᑐᕐᑲᐃᑦ ᐅᓂᒃᑳᖅᓯᒪᔪᑦ ᐅᑭᐅᖅᑕᖅᑐᒥ ᓇᐹᖅᑐᖅᑲᖅᑕᓚᐅᕐᓂᖕᒐᓂᒃ ᐊᒻᒪᓗ ᐊᐱᑦᑕᕐᓂᖕᒐᓂᒃ ᐱᖕᒐᖕᓇᒥ. ᐃᓐᓇᑐᕐᑲᐃᑦ ᐅᓂᒃᑳᖅᓯᒪᒋᑦᑐᑎᒃ ᐃᒃᐲᓇᓕᖅᐸᓪᓕᐊᓂᖕᒐᓂᒃ ᓯᓚᐅᑉ ᓇᐹᖅᑐᐃᓪᓗ ᐆᒪᒍᓐᓇᐃᓪᓕᒐᒥᒃ ᐱᕈᕈᓐᓇᑐᐃᓐᓇᓕᖅᑐᑦ ᐱᖕᒐᖕᓇᒥ. ᐅᑭᐅᖅᑕᖅᑐᒥᓗ ᐊᐱᑦᑕᓕᖅᓗᓂ ᑲᓇᖕᓇᒥ. ᐃᒃᐲᓈᓗᕐᑲᑦᑕᕐᓂᖕᒐᓄᑦ ᓇᓄᕐᓄᑦ ᑎᑭᑕᐅᑦᑕᓕᕐᓂᖅᓗᓂ. ᐃᒃᐲᓇᓕᖅᐸᓪᓕᐊᓪᓗᓂ ᐃᒃᐲᓇᕐᓂᖅᐹᒍᑦ ᑎᑭᓐᓇᒥ, ᐅᖅᑰᓯᕚᓪᓕᐊᓕᓇᓪᓗᓂ. ᑕᐃᒪᓐᓇ ᐱᓪᓗᒍ ᓇᓄᐃᑦ ᓇᔪᐃᓐᓇᕐᓂᖅᓴᐅᓪᓗᑎᒃ. ᑕᐃᒪᓕ ᓇᓄᐃᑦ ᓄᓇᓕᖕᓄᑦ ᑎᑭᑉᐸᓪᓕᐊᑦᑕᓕᖅᑯᑦ. ᐃᓛᓐᓂᒃᑯᑦ ᐱᖕᒐᓯᐃᒻᒪᕆᒃᓗᑎᒃ ᓄᓇᓕᖕᓄᑦ ᓇᓄᐃᑦ ᑎᑭᑦᑕᓕᖅᑯᑦ. ᐅᕐᑲᓗᒻᕖᒃᑯᑦ ᓇᓄᕐᑲᓕᕋᐃᖕᒪᑦ ᓇᓗᓇᐃᕈᑎᕐᑲᓕᖅᓗᓂ. ᓄᓇᓕᖕᒥᐅᑦ ᓄᑕᕋᐃᑦ ᐅᓐᓄᒃᑯᑦ ᐊᖕᒋᕐᕋᖅᓯᒪᒋᐊᕐᑲᓕᖅᓗᑎᒃ 10:00 -ᒧᐊᕐᕌᖕᒐ, ᓇᓄᕐᓄᑉ ᐱᔭᐅᕐᑯᓇᒋᑦ. ᑕᐃᒪᓕ ᐅᖅᑰᓯᒃᑲᕐᓂᕐᒪᑦ ᓇᐹᖅᑐᐃᑦ ᐅᑎᓕᒃᑲᕐᓂᕆᕗᑦ ᐊᒻᒪᓗ ᓇᓄᕐᑲᕈᓐᓃᖅᓗᓂ. ᑲᖕᒍᐃᑦ ᐊᕐᕌᒍᓗᒃᑖᖅ ᓇᔪᖅᐸᓕᓇᓪᓗᑎᒃ ᐊᒻᒪᑦᑕᐅᖅ ᑐᒃᑐᑎᑐᑦ. ᐅᖅᑰᓗᐊᕐᓂᖕᒐ ᐱᓪᓗᒍ ᐃᓄᐃᑦ ᕐᑲᓪᓗᓈᑦ ᓄᓇᖕᒐᓐᓄᑦ ᓅᒋᐊᕐᑲᓕᖅᐳᑦ, ᐃᒃᐲᓇᖅᐸᓪᓕᐊᓂᖕᒐ ᑕᐃᑲᓂ ᐱᔾᔪᑎᒥᓪᓗᒍ, ᐊᒻᒪᓗ ᐊᓪᓚᐃᑦᓅᒋᐊᕐᑲᓕᓇᓪᓗᑎᒃ ᑲᓇᖕᓇᒧᑦ ᐅᑭᐅᖅᑕᖅᑐᒧᑦ, ᑕᐃᑲᓂ ᐅᖅᑰᓂᖅᓴᐅᓂᖕᒐ ᐱᔾᔪᑕᐅᓪᓗᓂ. ᐅᑭᐅᖅᑕᖅᑐᖅ ᐅᖅᑯᓪᓗᓂ ᐱᕈᖅᑐᓕᒃᔪᐊᖖᒍᖅᐳᖅ ᒪᖕᒐᑭᑯᓗᖕᓂᒃ ᐱᑕᕐᑲᓕᖅᓗᓂ ᓂᕚᖕᒐᔪᓂᒃ. ᐱᖕᒐᖕᓇᒥ ᐅᑭᐅᖅᑕᖅᑐᓕᒃᑐᑦ ᑕᐃᒪᐃᓕᖅᓗᓂ. ᓇᓄᐃᑦ ᓇᒥᑐᐃᓐᓈᓕᖅᑯᑦ. ᐱᖕᒐᖕᓇᒥ ᐃᓄᐃᑦ ᐊᒻᒪᓗ ᐅᑭᐅᖅᑕᖅᑐᒥ ᐆᒪᔪᕐᑯᑏᑦ ᐊᓕᐊᓇᐃᒍᓯᓕᖅᐳᑦ ᐃᒃᐲᓇᖅᑐᒦᒍᓐᓇᓕᕋᒥᒃ. ᑲᓇᖕᓇᒥᓕ ᐊᓪᓚᐃᑦ ᐊᒻᒪᓗ ᐱᖕᒐᖕᓇᒥᐅᑦ ᑲᔾᔮᖅᓗᑎᒃ ᐅᖅᑰᒍᓐᓇᕋᒥ. ᐊᕐᕌᒍᑦ 100-ᑦ ᓈᑦᑕᕌᖕᒐᑕ ᑲᓇᖕᓇᖅ ᐊᒻᒪᓗ ᐱᖕᒐᖕᓇᖅ ᐊᓯᔾᔨᖅᐸᒃᓗᑎᒃ ᓯᓚᒥᒃ. ᐊᕐᕌᒍᑦ ᓇᓕᐊᑦ ᐅᖅᑰᓂᖅᓴᐅᑦᑕᖅᓗᓂ ᐅᕝᕙᓘᓐᓃᑦ ᐃᒃᐲᓇᕐᓂᖅᓴᐅᑦᑕᖅᓗᓂ. ᓇᒦᒻᒪᖕᖔᖅᐱᑦ ᒪᓕᖅᓗᓂ.

The Legend of the North and South

Kukik Tagalik

Elders used to say there used to be trees in the North and snow around the South. They say it got colder over the years and the trees all died off and started to grow down south. Snow started to fall in the North. It got so cold in the North the polar bears started to come. As soon as it got to its coldest point, it started to get warmed. This made the polar bears stay longer.

The polar bears came into town. They came into town at least three times a day. There was even a polar bear hotline. The kids in town had to be home by 10:00 pm, so the polar bears would not get them.

After it got warm again the trees came back and the polar bears left. The geese stayed all year long as well as the caribou. It got so hot that the Inuit had to move to the South where it was getting colder and the Indians had to move north where it was warm enough for them. The North was turning into a jungle with little monkeys hanging around.

In the South it was turning into a winter wonderland. Polar bears were everywhere. In the South the Inuit and the Indians and the southern animals were happy to be in the warmth.

Every hundred years the South and the North changed weather. Each year it is getting warmer or colder. It depends where you are.

⊲ˢᐅⵠⴰᑕ	Arviat
∩ᑭᔪˤ᛭⊲ˤᑊ	Whale Cove
ᑲ᷎∩ˤᑊⵠᒍᓂˤᑊ	Rankin Inlet
ᑭᵃᵃᒪᗝᐃᑕ	Cape Dorset
ᐃˤᑲᗝᐃᑕ	Iqaluit
ᐸᵃᓂˤᑲᒌ	Pangnirtung
ᓇᓂᔭᐁᑲ	Nanisivik
ᒪᑕᑎᒪᑕᒍᑊ	Pond Inlet
ᐃᑲᐱᐁˤᑊ	Arctic Bay
ˤᑲᐅᑭᐃᑕᗝˤᑊ	Resolute Bay
⊲ᑲᐅᐃᑕᗝˤᑊ	Grise Fiord

ᑎᑭᖅᕐᕈᐊᖅ
ᐃᓄᒡᓚᒃ ᐃᓕᓐᓂᐊᕐᕕᖕᓯ

Whale Cove
Inuglak School

ᑎᑭᖅᕐᕇᐊᕐ ᕼᐊᒪᓚᖕᓯ ᑎᑭᖅᕇᑦᑐᖅ ᑲᓇᑕᐅᑉ ᓄᓇᕐᕙᖕᓗᓂᖅ ᑲᖕᒋᖅᐸᒃᕋᒎᒃ ᑎᑭᖅᕙᖕᑕ ᐃᓲᐊᖓ, ᐊᒻᓗ 400-ᓂᖅ ᐃᓄᓕᒃᑲᑎᒃᑐᓂ. ᑖᓐ ᓄᓇᑲᑕᕇᖅ ᑲᑎᖕᖃᐅᑦᑐᖅᑐᖅ ᖁᐸᓗᒡᓯᓄᒃ, ᐊᒻᓗ ᓇᓄᒃᓄᒃ ᐊᖅᑯᑎᐅᒎᒃᓄ ᐃᖕᒋᖅᕋᖅᕘᓇᑕ. ᖃᖅᑲᒃᕐᖃᐅᖅᒎᒃᓄ, ᓯᐅᒃᖅᑲᐅᖅᒎᒃ, ᑕᓯᕐᖃᐅᖅᒎᒃ ᐊᒻᓗ ᑰᖅᑲᐅᖅᒎᒃ ᓇᖅᕼᓂᒎᓪᓗ. ᐊᐅᔭᒥ, ᐃᓚᖕᖃᓂᒃᒡᑕᓐᒃ ᓯᓚᑐᖅᖃᖅᑎᑦᑐᒃ, ᐊᒻᓗ ᐊᐱᐊᒃᒎᒃ ᐊᒃᒎᐱᓐᒥ. ᓯᑦᕿᓕᕐᑦᓂᖕᓯ ᐱᐊᑦᒎᔪ, ᓇᑎᑭᕐᐊᕐᕆᑦᒎᖅ ᐊᐱᓕᐊᑦᒎᓂᒎᓪᓗ.

ᐃᓄᒡᓚᒃ ᐃᓕᓐᓂᐊᕐᕕᖕᓯ K-11-ᒎᒃ ᐃᓕᓐᓂᐊᕐᕕᐊᐅᕐᕘᖅ. ᐃᓕᓐᓂᐊᑎᐊᑎᕇᖅᑦᑐᑎᒃ ᐱᓕᔾᕙᔪᓄᒃ ᐳᖅᑐᓂᕐᒎᒃ, ᐃᓕᓐᓂᐊᑦᑐᑎ ᐃᓕᓐᓂᐊᖅᑎᑕᐅᕐᒃᑦᑐᑎᒃ ᓇᖕᒋᓂᖅ ᐅᖃᐅᓯᖕᒪᖕᒃ ᐊᑐᖅᑕᐅᕋᒎ ᐃᓄᒃᑎᑐᑦ.

The hamlet of Whale Cove is situated on a long point of the Canadian mainland that projects into Hudson Bay, and has a population of 400. This community is a congregational point for beluga whales, and it is also on the seasonal polar bear migration route. Whale Cove is covered in rolling hills, wild coastal beaches, lakes and rivers, and tundra valleys. In the summer, there is sometimes rain, and snow begins to accumulate in October. Because of the strong winds in this community, huge snowdrifts often occur.

Inuglak School is a K–11 school. From kindergarten to third grade, students study in their native language, Inuktitut.

ᐊᑎᖅᖁᑎᑕᐅᒪᕐᑕᒍᕐᑉ

ᕙᐅᑐᓕᐊ ᓇᐸᔪᖅ, ᒍᓴᑦ 8

ᐅᐱᕐᖏᑕᐅᒐ ᐅᖓᕐᑫᑕᑦ ᓄᓇᓕᓗᒐᑎᓂ ᑲᖕᖅᕐᔭᕐᖁᓐ ᐃᓱᐊᓂ ᕼᐊᕐᓇᐊ ᐱᒐ. ᑎᖕᒥᐊᑦ ᑐᖕᓴᐅᑕᓐᑐᓐᑎ. ᐊᓄᕆᖅᖁᕐᑎᓂ ᐊᒻᒪ ᐊᑐᐅᑐᖃᕐᓴᒐ. ᓯᖁᒥᓴᓐᑕᐊᕐᔭᓯᓂ; ᓱᖃ ᖁᑲᐅᓕᓐᑐᓂ ᑐᖁᒃᕋᓯᓂ. ᐊᒥᓗᑭᓕᐊᑦ ᑲᑎᕙᖃᐳᑦ ᐃᐅᓕᒐᔮᕐᑦᑦ ᑕᑕᓕᐅᑦᒥᓯᖅ ᖃᕐᐃᓴᓯᑎᒐᐅᕐᕐᓂᓂ. ᐊᕐᖁᕐᑦᖕᕐ ᓐᕐᐊᑐᔪᐊᐦ ᑐᖕᓴᕐᐃᕐᖁᐦᖀ ᓯᐅᓯ ᓐᖀᓐᕐᐅᕐᕆ ᐊᒐᓯᕐᐦ. ᐊᑎᐆᓕᓯᑦ ᕐᐦᑐᖕᖀᑕᐅᕐᖁᐸᖒᒃᐱᐅᓯᕐᓂᑕ ᐦᕐᑐᖕᐊᐦᕐᖁᒃᐆᓐᐊᓂᑦ. ᑳᑐᖕᖁᓕᑦᑦ ᐃᐅᐊᕐᓂᓄ ᐅᖒᐊᑎᒐᐆᕐᐃᐦ ᑕᑦᑦᒃᑲᒃ ᐅᕐᖁᖕᐆᑦ ᕐᐦᓂᕐᕐᕐᐊᐦ ᐅᕐᖁᖕᐅᕐᑐᓯ ᐊᒻᓗ ᐊᕐᐱᑦᐆᒐ ᖁᕐᐃᐊᓗ. ᒍᓪᐊᓐᐊ ᐊᒻᓗ ᕐᐃᐊᓗ ᖁᐊᕐᑦᐦᐃ ᑎᑕᒐᔪᐊᑦᖒᒃᑲᑦ ᐅᖒᐊᑎᐊᕐᖕᕐ, ᐱᕆᐆᓇᒃ ᒍᓪᐊᓐᐊ ᐅᕐᖁᐆᓯᐦᐆ, "ᐃᕐᖁᐆᓕᐃᕐᐦ ᐅᐱᕐᒃᐆᐆᑲᕐᒃ ᐊᖕᑦᕐᖕᖁᖕᐃᓂᐆᓐᐅ ᐅᕐᖁᕐᑕᐅᕐᓕᐊᒐᕐᖀ?"

"ᕐᐊᐆᑦ ᐅᐆᕐᖁᐆᑐᖕᖀᐦ?" ᐊᐱᕆᓐᐆᓐᒍᕐ."

"ᐅᐆᕐᖁᐆᑐᖕᖀᐆ ᐅᕐᖁᖅᕐᖁᐃᕐᐆᓕᒐᐃᐆ ᕐᐃᐆᐸᕐ ᐊᕐᕐᐃᐆᕐᕐᐆᓂᒃᐆᕐ ᑎᑐᕐᐊᕐᖁᖒᕐᑐᐆᑎᑦᑦᓂᐆ ᓐᐃᐦᓂᐆ᐀ᐆᐅᒃᑎᐦ ᐃᐆᐆᐊᕐᒃᐆᑦ."

ᐅᕐᖁᒍᕐᓯᑦ ᐱᑭᐆᓐᒍᑐᕐ, "ᐃᐆᓯᓂᐊᕐᖁᕐᕐᖁᐆᑦᐆᐆᐊᓂᐆᖒᐦᐆᑦ ᓐᐃᐆᕐᐆᓐᓯᕐᒐᐆᐆ ᐃᐆᐆᐊᕐᓂᓂᓐᕐᐆᓂ."

ᑕᐆᓪ ᓐᐃᒍᐆᕐᒍᓐᒍ ᐅᖒᐊᑎᒐᕐᖕᕐ ᑕᐆᐃᕐᐆᑎᐊᕐᓂᐆᐆᕐ ᕐᐃᐆ ᐊᕐᕐᐃᕐᐆᖒᕐᒃᐦ. ᕐᐃᐆᐊᐆᑐᐆᕐᒃᐆᐆᑎ ᐊᒻᓗ ᐊᖕᖕᐊᕐᐃᐆᐆᕐᒃᐆᐆᑎ.

ᕼᐊᐆᒐᕐᒥᐆ ᑐᕐᓯᕐᒐᕐᑦ ᓂᐆᓯᖕᖅᕐᑐᐆᐆᑦ ᖃᕐᐱᐆᐆᐆᐃᑦᐆᐆᑐᕐᒃᐆᐆᕐᒃᐆᒃᐆᒃᐦᑐᐆᑦ, "ᕼᐁᐆ, ᐃᐆᕐᕆᕐᖁᕐᐅᐆᑕᑦᑦᑦ!" ᑕᐆᕐᒃᐆᐆᕐᒃᐦᒃᐆᒃᐆᐆᐆ ᖃᕐᐃᐆᐆᕐᒃᐆᕐᒃᐆᕐᒃᐆᐆᒃᐆᕐᐆᓂ, ᑕᐆᕐᒃᐆᕐᒃᐦᐆᕐᒃᐆᒃᐆᒃᐆᓂᕐᐆᐦ.

ᒍᓪᐊᓐᐊ ᐅᕐᖁᕐᕆᕐᐆᑎ ᐅᕐᖁᕐᒐᕐᒃᐆᐆᕐᓂᐆᑦ, "ᑕᐆᕐᕆᕐᐆᑦ, ᐅᕐᖁᐆᕐᐆᑎᐆᖒᒃᐆᐆᐅᕐᓯᐆᐆᒃ. ᐅᖒᐊᑎᒐᐆᕐᕐᓂᐃᐆ ᐅᕐᖁᐆᕐᖕᕐᐅᕐᒃᐆᐃᐆ ᐃᐆ ᐱᐆᐱᕐᓯᐆᐊᕐᒃᐆᕐᐦ."

ᑕᐆᓪᒐᐆᓇ ᐊᑦᐆᕐᒃᐆᑦ ᐅᕐᖁᕐᕐᐆᐆᑎᐆᓐᐆᕐᐆᐦ, ᐊᒻᓗ ᒍᓪᐊᓐᐊᕐ ᐅᕐᖁᕐᒃᐆᕐᒃᐆᐆᑦᐆᖒᕐ ᒪᐆᓐᒃᐆᐆᐆ, ᕐᐃᐆ ᐱᐆᐱᕐᓯᐆᕐᒃᐆᓐᐆᕐ. ᑕᐆᕐᒃᐆᐃᐆᐆᐆᐆᓄᓐᐆᐆᕐᕐᓂᐆᒃᐆᒃᐆᐆᕼᐊᐆᒐᕐᒃᐆᐆᕐᐆᐃᐆᐆᐆ. ᖃᕐᐃᐆᐆᓐᐆᕐ ᐊᕐᖕᕐᐆᕐᒃᐆᐆᑦᐆᓐᐆᐆᑐᐆᓐᐆᒃᐆ. ᑕᐆᓪᐆᖒᓂᐆᓐᐆ ᓂᐆᐆᐃᐆᐆᕐᒃᐆᕐᐆᐆᐦᕐᒃᐆ ᓐᐆᕐᕐᐆᐆᕐᒃᐆᖒᐆᐆᕐᐆᓂᐆᐆᐆᑦᐆᕐᐆᐆ ᐃᐆᐆᐊᕐᒃᐆᐆ᐀ᐆᕐᒃᐆᐆᐆᑦ.

ᐃᕐᐊ.

Untitled

Andrea Napayok, Grade 8

It was a warm spring morning in a little town near Hudson Bay.

Birds were singing. The wind was calm and no one was out. The sun was shining brightly; the sky was bright and blue.

I looked around at all the homes and all the windows were still closed. It was very peaceful.

All of a sudden the birds stopped singing. The wind started to blow fiercely, and clouds covered the sky.

I ran inside and asked Gloria and Shelley Anne to come over. When they came we talked about going to the graveyard because we were bored. We started walking and while we were walking we picked colourful stones.

Then, when we finally got to the graveyard we saw this beautiful ring. It had little colourful diamonds around it and a big diamond in the middle. Gloria, Shelley-Anne, and I decided to take the ring, but Gloria said, "You know that myth our parents told us?"

"What myth?" we asked.

"The myth about the weather changing when we steal from a grave."

We said, "They're just trying to teach us not to steal from graves."

So we took the ring and in a matter of seconds the weather changed. It started raining very hard and the wind picked up.

We heard a Honda so we started yelling, "Hey, help us!" The person saw us and started coming toward us, but it became very foggy.

Gloria said to us, "See, I told you guys. Maybe if we put the ring back it'll clear up."

So that's what we did and, just like Gloria said, it began to clear up. We could now see the person driving the Honda. He came to us and gave us a ride home. From then on we girls never took a thing from a grave.

THE END

ᐊᓂᕐᓂᖅ ᑐᕐᖃ ᑕᛕᐊᓂᒥ

ᓯᐊᑕ ᐊᓐ ᕗᐃᓯ

ᔭᕐᐊ 04 ᐅᖕᓗᖕᒥ, ᐊᖅᓱᓇᓯᕐᐊᐅᖅᖁᒡᔪᔾ ᑐᕐᖃ ᑕᒐᔾᔪᖓ. ᖄᑲᐃᖕᕿᕐᕹᕝ 13 ᒪᐃᓚᓂᑦ ᐅᖁᕙᖃᑎᒃᑎᓂ ᖓᔪ ᓄᓚᕐᕿᐊᒻᓂ. ᑖᐃᑲᕋᖕ ᐊᖅᒃᑎᐊᑐ, ᓇᓯᖕᕿᒃ ᑖᑐᓗᑦᑦ, ᖝᑊᐱᕿᕐᓗᖕ ᖝᑊᐱᕐᑐᐅᕝᑦᑦ ᖝᑊᓇᕝᕼᐊᒡᔾ. ᓇᑊᐱᖕᒡᔭ, ᐊᑊᒃᑐᖅᑊᑲ, ᐱᐱᕐᒡᔪ. ᖝᑊᒡᓗᔾ ᑖᑐᕐᕹᕝᑲ ᑕᒐᔾᖓ ᑐᕐᖃ. ᖝᑊᒡᓗᔾ ᖝᕿᐊᐅᑊᖃᕐᒡᓕ ᑲᑕᙱᔾᑲ ᑖᑐᕐᓂᔾᐅᓗ.

ᐊᖕᑐᖓᐊ ᐅᖅᑊᖓᕐᖓ, "ᐱᓚᕐᒃᕿᐊᖅᑊᕌᕝᕜ ᓄᑐᖕᒃᕜ ᐹᕈᐳᖕᕿᕐᒡᔮᒃᔾ." ᓄᑐᖕᑕᔾᕜ ᐹᕈᐳᖕᕿᕐᐅᓂᑊᔾᖓ, ᐊᖕᑊᐅᓯᕐᒡᓕ ᒪᕼᖑᒃᐱᒐ ᐅᙱᑊᕐᕛᕼᕜ ᐊᒃᐱᒃᕿᕝᕜ ᐊᖃᒃᕼᒻᕜ ᑕᕝᕼᖃᕝᑐᕝᒡᕜ ᑐᔾᑐᑊᐊᓐᐊᕗᕈᓂᔾᐊᒡ. ᐊᖕᑐᖓᐊᔾ ᐅᖅᑊᓗ ᑕᒐᕝᕜ ᐱᔾᖓᕿᕐᕿᓛᓂᒡ ᑐᔾᑐᖕᐳᒡᔭ. ᐱᐊᓚᕐᕹᕼᒡᓕ ᑐᔾᑐᕝᕜ ᐊᖃᑐᓯᕐᖓ. ᐊᖕᕼᕋᕛᕼᕜ ᐅᕈᓚᖅᑊᒡᔾ ᐱᑕᕼᕹᕐᖃᑊᕟᓐᖕᒃ. ᐊᖕᕼᕋᕛᕜ ᒪᐃᐊᒃᔾ

ᐅᔾᕜᒡᔾᖓ. ᐃᔾᕼᕿᒐᕼ ᐊᖕᑐᖓᐊ ᐅᖅᑊᖓᕐᖓ, "ᓂᓕᕼᖃᐅᕜᒐᒪ ᐃᓄᖄᕼᕼᔾᕼᕜᒃ."

"ᐅᕜᕼᕼᓗ," ᐅᖅᑊᓗ ᕿᐅᑊᓗ.

ᐅᐊᓗᒥ ᓯᕼᖓᕼᑲᔮᒡᑊᖓ ᐊᓂᕐᓂᕐᓄᖃ ᐅᕼᖃᑎᐅᑊᖓ. ᐃᓄᖄᕼᕿᕜᖕᑑ ᑕᐅᑐᑐᕼᕼᕜᒻᖅᔮᕼ. ᐊᓂᕐᓂᕼ ᐅᕜᖃᕼ ᐅᖃᐅᕼᔾᕜᖃᖓ ᐊᕛᕼᔾᐊᕼᕜᖃᕼ ᑐᔾᑐᖃᕼᐊᒐᔾᕼᖓ.

ᕿᐅᕜᒡᔾ, "ᐱᓚᕼᕿᕜᕼ ᐃᓕᖃᕼᑲᕜ ᐱᖓᑎᐊᖃᕼᒡᔮᒃ."

ᐊᓂᕐᓂᐅᕼᕜᕜ ᐅᖅᑊᖓᕝᖓ, "ᑕᖃᖃᕼᕼᖓ ᐊᕜᕼᕼᕼᒐᑎᕼᐊᕼᒡᕜᒡᕼ ᐱᓚᕼᕼᐊᕼᕼ<ᕜᕼᒐᕼᖓᕜ."

"ᖃᕼᐅᕼᕜ ᐊᕜᕼᖓᕼᒐᕼᕼᖓ>ᕜᕼᕼ?" ᐊᕼᐱᓂᕜᕜ.

ᐊᓂᕐᓂᐅᕼᕜᕜ ᕿᐅᕜᒡᕜᖓᕜ, "ᐃᒪᕼᖓᕼ." ᐊᕜᕿᕼᕜᕼᖓᕜ ᐊᕼᐅᕼᕿᕼ ᓯᕜᕼᕼᒡᕼᕼᒡ ᐳᔮᒡᕜ. ᐊᕼᕜᐊᕼᒡᕜ ᐊᕼᐅᕼᕜᕼᖓ ᕼᕜᓯᕜᕼᒡᕜᖓᕼ.

ᕼᕜᒥᕜᒡᖓᕜᕼ ᖂᔮᕼᐅᕜᕼᒡᕜ ᐃᕼᓕᕼᕹᕼᐊᕼᕿᕼᕜᖓᕼ. 21

ᐊᓂᕐᓂᐅᕼᕜᕜ ᐅᕼᖃᑎᕜᕜᖓᕜ, "ᕿᐅᕜᕼᕜᖓᕼ ᓂᕼᕼᔾᐊᒡᕜᔾ ᕿᕜᕿᕼᕼ ᔾᕜ ᐊᕼᖃᕼᕜᕜᕼᕝ."

ᕿᐅᕜᕼᕼᓗ ᕿᐅᕜᒡᔾ, "ᓂᕼᕼᔾᕼᕼᕿᖓᕼᕜᕼᕜᕜᖓᕼ ᐊᓂᕐᓂᕼᕼᕜᕜ, ᒡᕜ ᕿᕜᐊᕼ ᓂᕼᕼᔾᕼᕜᒡᕜᕜᒡ. ᔾᕼᖃᕜᒡᕜᕜ ᐃᕼᓕᕼᕜᕼᕜ ᑐᕼᖃᕜᕜᖓᕜ.

ᐅᕼᒡᐊᕼᕜᕜ ᑕᑕᕿᕜᕿᕜ ᔾᕜᕜᕜᕜ. ᐊᕼᐅᕼᕿᕼᕜᒡᔾᕜᕼᕜᖓᕜ ᔾᕜᕜᕼᕜᒡᕜᕼᕜᖓᕜ. ᐅᕼᖃᕼᕜᒡᔾ "ᐅᕼᐊᕼᕜᕜᕟ! ᔾᕼᕜᕼᕜᒡᕜᕜ ᔾᕜᕼᕼᕜ! ᐅᕼᖃᕼᕜᕼᐱᕼᕜᕼᕜᒡᕜ ᔾᕼ ᓄᕼᕜᕼᕼᕜᕜ ᐅᕼᖃᕼᕜᕼᑑᕼᕼ ᖃᕼᐊᕼᕼᕜᕿᕼᕜ ᐅᕼᖃᕼᕼ ᐊᕼᕜᕼᕜᒡᕜᖓ. ᐊᕼᕼᕼᕜᕼᕼᕜ ᕼᕜᕿᕼᕼᕜᕿᑎᒪᕼᕜ ᖃᕼᕼᒡᕜ, ᐊᕼᕿᕼᐱᕼᕼᕜᒡᕼᕼᕜᕜ ᐃᕼᓕᕼᕼᕼᕼᕜ ᓇᕼᕜᕼᐊᕼᕜᕜᕼᕜᒡᕜ. ᑕᐊᕼᕜᕜ ᕼᕜᕿᕼᑐᕼᕹᕼᕟ ᐃᕼᕜᕼᕼᒡᕼᕼᕼᕼᕜᕜᒡᕜ. ᒍᕜᕼᐊᕼ ᐅᕼᖃᕼᕼᐹᕼᕜᕜᒡᔾ, "ᔾᕼᕜᒡᕼ ᑐᕼᕼᔾᕼᐊᕼᕜᕼᕜ ᔾᕜ ᐱᐊᕼᕿᕼᒡᕜᒡᕼᕜ." ᔾᕼᕜᕿᕼᕿᕼᕜᕜ ᒍᕼᕜᕜ ᐊᕼᕟᓗ ᑐᕼᕼᔾᕼᕼᕹᕜᕜᕜ ᖃᕼᐅᕼᕼᕿᕼᒡᕜ. ᐅᕼᕜᕼᕜ ᑐᕼᕜᕟᐊᕼᕜ ᔾᕼᕟᑊᓂᕼᕼᕹᕼᐅᕼᕜᕼᕟᕼᕿᕼᒡᕜ. <ᕼᖃᕼᕜᕜᕜᕟᕜ ᐅᕼᕿᕼᒡᕼᔾᕼᕜ ᔾᕜ ᓄᕼᕜᕼᕼᕜᕟᕜ, ᐊᕟᕼᓗ ᕿᕟᕼᔾᕼᐊᕼᓂᕼ ᐃᕼᕜᕟᕼᕿᕼᒡᔾᕜᒡᕜᕜᕜᕜ.

ᐃᕟᕜᐊ!

The Spirits of Turgeon Lake

Shelley Anne Voisey

On the fourth day of July, we went out camping to Turgeon Lake. Our camping site was thirteen miles away from Bure City. On the way to Turgeon Lake, we saw a seal, I took my rifle and shot it in the neck. I took it with a niksik, cut it up, and stored it. I looked ahead and saw Turgeon Lake. As I looked I saw a herd of caribou. Andrea said, "We'll chase them after we have tea and bannock."

When we were done having tea and bannock, I took my camouflage suit and headed for the herd of caribou. Andrea and I caught three each. I took out my knife and started to cut our caribou. The other caribou started at us and took off. We went home and cooked some of our meat. We put the rest of the meat in the boat. The cooking was done and Andrea said, "After I eat I am going to bed." "So will I," I said.

In the night I dreamt about spirits haunting me. They looked like inukpasugjuks. The spirits told me we caught too many caribou.

I said, "We caught only three each."

The spirits said, "You are going to be stuck here for a week or so."

"How am I going to be stuck here?" I asked.

The spirits said, "With this." They threw a windy and rainy pouch. It was really windy and rainy. You could have had a shower outside.

The spirits said, "Only if you worship us will we fix the weather."

I told them, "I don't worship spirits, I only worship God." My dream ended and I woke up.

I looked out the door. It was really windy and rainy. I said, "MY GOSH! My dream came true!" I tried calling Bure City but the aerial got wet so the high frequency blew up. It went in a thousand pieces, and I tried to put them back, but some of the pieces got lost. So I went back and looked at my dream. I said to Gloria, "Let's all pray to God for the weather to clear up." We started praying to God and he answered our prayers. The next day the weather cleared up. We packed and headed for Bure City, and lived happily ever after.

The End!

Untitled

Tanya Kritaquluk, Grade 7

It was a beautiful spring night. The blue stars in the sky were so bright and glowed like fireflies. The moon was brightly shining on the bay ice. The moon and the stars were moving slowly. The moon was very bright—it was trying to tell me that it was past twelve o'clock.

I was thinking something. I lay down and looked at the stars. I saw a falling star and I wished to see a mermaid.

I heard a voice that was so soft. I looked around. I saw Sedna the mermaid. She had blue eyes, long purple hair, red lips, and a small nose. She was talking to me, telling me what it was like living under the sea.

I started to tease her about her half-human and half-fish body. She got mad and started to say her magic words, "Aja jajajajaja nukanguuq ajunqissalirit aijajaja." The terrible wind was coming. The terrible wind was the strongest that I've ever seen. The waves got rough and crashed to the rocks. When the sand hit, it hurt.

I asked Sedna to stop the storm because she scared me to death. So I asked her to accept my apology. Then she accepted it. The weather cleared up. I was really happy.

We didn't have anything to say, so I started walking. I looked at the beach. She disappeared. I went home.

When I went home, I fell asleep because I was too tired. When I woke up, I looked out my window. The sun was really bright and I knew that I had to go out and enjoy my day.

ᐊᑎᕐᑲᖅᑎᑕᐅᙱᑦᑐᖅ

ᑖᓂᐊ ᕐᑭᑕᕐᑯᓗᒃ, ᒍᕇᑦ 7

ᐅᐱᕐᖔᒥ ᓯᓚᑦᑎᐊᕙᐅᔪᐸᓘᑦᑐᓂ ᐅᓐᓂᐊᒃᑯᑦ. ᐅᑦᑐᓇᐊᑦ ᑐᖑᔪᖅᑐᒥᒃ ᑕᐅᑦᑐᕐᑲᐅᖅᓱᑎᒃ ᕐᑲᐅᒪᔪᐊᓗᐃᑦ ᑕᑯᒃᓴᐅᑦᑎᐊᖅᓱᑎᒃ. ᑕᖅᑭᐅᑉ ᕐᑲᐅᒪᓂᖓ ᕐᑲᐅᒪᑦᑐᓂ ᑲᖏᖅᓘᑉ ᓯᑯᖓᓄᑦ. ᑕᖅᑭᖅ ᐅᑦᑐᓇᐊᑦᑐ ᓲᒃᑲᐃᑦᑐᒥᑦ ᐃᖏᕐᕋᑦᑐᑎᒃ. ᑕᖅᑭᖅ ᕐᑲᐅᒪᔪᐸᓘᑦᑐᓂ— ᓱᓇᒥᑭᐊᖅ ᐅᕙᓐᓄ ᕐᑲᐅᔨᒃᑲᐃᓐᓇᓱᒃᑲᒥᕐᑲᐃ ᑐᐊᔪ ᐅᖓᑖᓄᑦ ᐅᓐᓄᖕᒪᑦ ᕐᑲᐅᔨᓴᐅᑎᒃᑯᑦ.

ᐃᓱᒪᐅᔭᓱᒐᒪ ᓱᓇᒥᑭᐊᖅ. ᓇᑦᓚᖓᑦᑐᖓ ᕐᑯᙱᐊᓕᖅᐳᖓ ᐅᑦᑐᓇᐊᓂᒃ. ᐅᑦᑐᓇᐊᒥᒃ ᐊᓇᖅᑐᒥᒃ ᑕᑯᒐᒪ ᐃᓱᒪᒋᔭᓐᓂᒃ ᐱᒍᒪᔭᓐᓂᒃ ᑕᑯᔪᒪᓕᖅᑯᖓ ᑕᑖᓕᔩᕐᒥᒃ.

ᓂᐱᒥᒃ ᓂᐱᑭᑦᑐᒥᒃ ᑐᓴᕋᒪ ᕐᑭᕕᐊᖅᓱᖓ ᑕᑯᒋᐊᓯᒍᖓ. ᓴᓐᓇ ᑕᑖᓕᔪᒥᒃ ᑕᑯᒍᖓ. ᐃᔨᖏᒃ ᑐᖑᔪᖅᓱᑎᒃ, ᓄᔭᖓᓗ ᐳᐴᑦᑐᓂ, ᐊᐅᐸᖅᑐᓂᒃ ᑲᒃᑭᕙᐊᕐᑲᖅᓱᓂ, ᐊᒻᒪᓗ ᕐᑭᖓᖓ ᒥᑭᑦᑑᑦᑐᓂ. ᐅᕙᓐᓄᑦ ᐅᕐᑲᒪᔩᖅ, ᕐᑲᓄᖅ ᐃᓅᓯᕐᒥᓂᒃ ᑕᕆᐅᑉ ᐊᑖᓂ.

ᒥᑖᕆᓇᓱᓕᖅᐸᕋ ᓇᑉᐸᖓᓂᒃ ᐃᓅᑉ ᑎᒥᖓᓂᒃ ᑎᒥᕐᑲᕐᓂᖓᓄᑦ ᓇᑉᐸᖓᓗ ᐃᕐᑲᓗᒃᑐᑦ ᐱᕐᑲᕐᓂᖓᓄᑦ. ᓂᙵᒃᓱᓂ ᐃᕆᓇᓕᐅᓕᖅᓱᓂ ᐃᒪᓐᓇ, "ᐊᔭ ᔭᔭᔭᔭᔭ ᓄᑲᙴᖅ ᐊᔪᕐᑭᔅᓴᓕᕆᑦ ᐊᔭᔭᔭ." ᐱᐅᙱᑦᑐᒥᒃ ᐊᓄᕆᓯᒍᖅ. ᐊᓄᕆ ᓴᙱᔪᒻᒪᕆᐊᓛᑦᑐᓂ ᑕᐃᒪᓐᓇᑐᑦ ᓴᙱᑎᒋᔪᒥᒃ ᑕᑯᓚᐅᖅᓯᒪᓇᖓ. ᑕᕆᐅᖅ ᒪᑦᓕᖅᑐᐊᓘᑦᓕᕐᒪᑦ ᐅᔭᕐᑲᓄᑦ ᐸᑎᒃᑕᓕᖅᓱᓂ.

ᓯᒡᔭᒧᑦ ᓯᐅᕋᕐᒧᑦ ᐱᑲᒻᒪᒐᐃᖕᒪᑦ, ᐋᓐᓂᖅᓇᖅᑐᐊᓘᑦᑐᓂ.

ᓴᓐᓇ ᑕᑖᓕᔩᖅ ᓄᖅᑲᕐᑯᑦᑐᒍ ᐅᕐᑲᐅᑎᔭᕋ ᑲᑉᐱᐊᓯᑦᑐᐊᓘᑦᓕᕐᒪᑦ. ᒪᒥᐊᓐᓂᕋᕋᒪ ᐅᕐᑲᐅᑎᒐᒃᑯ ᐊᖏᖅᓱᓂ. ᓯᓚᓗ ᐱᐅᓯᑦᑐᓂ. ᕐᑯᕕᐊᑦᑐᐹᔪᔪᖓ.

ᐅᕐᑲᐅᓯᒃᓴᕐᑲᙱᓐᓇᒪ, ᐱᓱᒋᐊᓕᖅᓱᖓ. ᓯᒡᔭ ᑕᑯᒋᐊᕐᑲᒃᑯ. ᐱᑕᕐᑲᔮᙱᑦᑐᖅ ᑕᑯᒃᓴᐅᓇᓂ. ᐊᖏᕐᕋᐅᑦᑐᖓ.

ᐊᖏᕐᕋᕋᒪ, ᓯᓂᓕᖅᓱᖓ ᑕᕐᑲᓯᒪᔪᐊᓘᒐᒪ. ᑐᐸᒃᑲᒪ, ᐃᒐᓛᒃᑯᑦ ᐃᑦᑐᐊᕋᒪ. ᓯᓚ ᓯᕐᑭᓐᓂᑦᑎᐊᖅᑐᖅ ᐊᒻᒪᓗ ᕐᑲᐅᔨᒪᑦᑐᖓ ᐅᑦᑐᕐᑲᑦᑎᐊᕐᓂᐊᕋᒪ.

ᑎᑎᕋᕐᔪᐊᖅ: ᐃᓄᒃᑕᒃ ᐃᓕᖅᓄᐊᕐᔪᖕᓇ

Untitled
Lenny Teenar, Grade 7

It was a beautiful afternoon. The sun was big and orange. It shone brightly on the hill and huge lake. I was fishing at a huge lake. It had a big fish. I started to get cold. There was a small Coleman stove. It had no gas for it.

When I got cold, I started to head back by walking. The Ski-Doo had no gas.

I saw a small cabin. I went there, and I saw a Coleman stove. I started the stove. I went outside and I saw a big storm. I went back in.

The storm broke the roof and the wall. I was so cold. I ran away from the storm. The storm was following. The storm took me and threw me to a hard ice. I hit my head. I lost a lot of blood.

I saw a polar bear den. I crawled inside. It was very dark and cold but it protected me from the storm. I stayed there a couple of days.

I heard a machine. I crawled out of the den. Rangers and hunters found me and took me back to the town.

ᐊᑎᖃᖅᓐᑕᐅᖅᒌᕐᑕᑐᖅ
ᓛᓂ ᑏᓇ, ᒍᓀᑦ 7

ᐅᓪᓗᑎᐊᕽᔪᑎᓐᑦᓲ ᓂᓚᓇᖅ ᖃᖅᕐᖅᠫᓚᓐᖅᑎᓐᑦᓲ. ᠫᖅᑕᖅ ᐊᐅᔭᐊᕽᑦᑖ ᑕᖅᖅᖅᖅᠫᑐ ᐊᖤᒌᖅᑿᔭᑦᓚᐨᓚ. ᖅᐃᖅᑐᐊᖅᕽᔭᑦ ᖅᐅᑦᓚᑐ ᐊᑦᓚᑐ ᑕᑦᐊᑐᐨᑦ ᐊᖅᕽᑕᐊᑐᐨᑦ. ᐃᖅᔭᖅᐱᓐ. ᐃᖅᐲᓇᖅᠫᕾᑕᖅᓚᑦ. ᐅᖅᔄᖯᐅᓐᑕᐅᓗᐊᖅ ᕾᐊᖅᔭᐅᓐᒌᖅ ᐅᖅᔪᖅᖅᖃᕾᑦᓚᑦ ᕾᕾᐊᓇ.

ᖅᕾᐅᑕᖅᓚ, ᐱᕾᖅᓚᖤ ᐊᖤᖅᕾᔭᑦ ᐅᓐᑎᐊᖅᓚᖤ. ᠫᕾᒑ ᖅᠫᑕᐅᕾᖅ ᐅᖅᠫᖅᕾᑕᕾᓇ.

ᑕᑦᓚᖤ ᐃᐢᐅᔮᕾᒌᖅ. ᑕᐃᑯᠫᓇᖅᒑ, ᕾᐊᖅᔭᐅᓂᕾ ᑕᑦᓚᖤ. ᐃᕾᕾᐊᖅᖯᑦ ᕾᐊᖅᔭᐅᓐ ᐃᕾᓲᒍ. ᠫᓚᒌᖅᒑ ᑕᑦᓚᖤ ᐱᖅᠫᓚᖯᖅᑑᐱᓀᐅᑐᐨᓲ. ᐃᓚᖅᖴᓇᓪᓚᖤ.

ᐊᓅᓐᐊᔪᐨᑦ ᐊᖁᓚ ᐊᑦᓚᐃᒌ ᐃᕾᔪᖦ ᖅᖴᓇ ᠫᕾᖅᓚᑐᐅ. ᐃᕾᖤᔭᖅᑦ ᐱᖅᑐᒌᑦ ᖅᕾᔪᑦᓚᖤ. ᐱᖅᑐᑦ ᒪᖅᕾᑕᐅᑐᐨᓲ. ᐊᓅᓐᒌ ᖴᐅᖯᐅᑐᐨᓲ ᠫᒍᑦ ᠫᐱᕾᔪᑦ. ᓇᖅᖅᑕᓚᖅᓚᖤ. ᐊᑦᖅᑐᐊᒍᖦᖅᓚᖤ. ᓇᐳᕻ ᠫᑎᠫᓚᓐᖯ ᑕᑯᑖᖁ. ᐃᓚᐊᐅᐊᔪᖤ. ᑖᖅᑐᐊᒍᑦ ᒌᓯᠫ ᐃᕾᕾᐊᔭᑐᓯᓲ ᕾᕾᐊᓯᕾ ᐱᖅᑐᒌᑦ ᖯᔭᖯᕾᑕᑦᓚᖤ. ᑕᐃᑯᓇ ᓇ᠖ᖅᖤᒍ ᐅᑐᐅᓐᖯ ᖅᕾᕾᓚᑦᓇᖅᖯ.

ᐊᐅᑕᐅᓐᖯ ᑐᖤᕾᒑ, ᐊᓇᑦᓚᖤ ᠫᓐᒌᑦ. ᖅᕾᓂᖅᓐᐅᑦ ᐊᖤᓇᕾᖦᓐᐅᑦᓲ ᓇᓂᔭᐅᑐᐨᓲ ᐊᖤᖅᕾᔭᐅᔭᐅᑐᐨᓲ ᓄᓇᑎᓐᐅᑦ.

Untitled

Bruce Teenar, Grade 9

It was a beautiful afternoon. The sun was big and yellow. It shone brightly on the land. I decided it was a great day for fishing.

The weather started to change. The sun was covered with dark grey clouds. The blizzard started from the north. I quickly went home. I heard from my mom that Lenny was lost so I went to look for him. I looked around Whale Cove. I found him near Police Lake. Lenny was very cold. I took him to my place. I gave him hot tea and blankets. I called everyone on the CB and told them I found him near Police Lake. Lenny was okay and I would take him home later.

The next day the blizzard stopped blowing. Lenny and I went fishing. The weather was very nice. Lenny and I also went caribou hunting. I killed two caribou and Lenny killed one. I talked to Lenny about the weather. If the weather comes from the north and west the weather is going to be very cold. If the weather is coming from the east and south it will be a nice day.

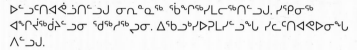

ᐊᏐᑦᖃᑦᕊᐳᑲᕐᑕᑐᖅ

ᐳᕽ Ꮒᓇ, ᒍᕆᕇ 9

ᐅᑐᑐᑎᐊᖁᒍᓐᕊᒍ ᓂᓇᕋᖅ ᖃᕊᑲᖃᕆᓓᕊᑎᕊᒍ. ᕍᕍᕋᖅ ᐊᕍᕆᕊᒃᒃᐿᕊᒍᓂ ᖄᖅᕊᕊᒍᓂ. ᐃᖅᕋᒃᕍᐳᕉᕆᕊᒍᕊ ᕍᓚᑎᐊᐊᐳᓇᕊ ᐱᓓᕊᒍ.

ᕍᓚ ᐊᕍᕆᕊᖅᕑᐊᕑᐊᕈᖅ. ᕍᕍᕋᖅ ᓯᕊᕌᓂᖅ ᑖᕉᑎᐊᑎᕊᒍᓂ. ᐱᖅᒍᕍᕆᕍᒪᕌᕊ ᑲᓇᕋᓕᕊ ᒍᐊᕍᕈ ᐊᕊᕆᕊᖅᐳᕈᒍ. ᐊᓐᒪᕌ ᐃᕊᐳᐱᕊᒍᓂᕊᓃ ᓂᓇᒍᖅ ᐊᕐᐳᕍᕌᕊ ᖄᕍᓂᐊᕍᕍᕍ. ᑎᐱᕊᕆᕍᕋᒍᕊᕝ ᖄᕊᓂᖄᕊᕑᕊᒍ. ᓇᓂᕊᒍ ᐳᕆᖅᕑᕊᒃᕐᕍᕊ ᑕᕍᕑᕌᕊ ᖄᕊᓂᕆᕊᕊᓚᕍ. ᓚᓂ ᖄᕍᐿᒃᕍᕊᕊᕊᕊ. ᐊᕊᕆᕊᖅᐳᕆᕊᒍᒍ. ᐃᕋᕊᒍᑖᕆᖅ ᐿᕍᕋᐳᕆᕊᒍᒍ ᐊᕌᕍᒍ ᖄᕆᕊᕌᕊᕑᕊᒍ. ᐃᕊᕋᕊᐲᕌᕈᕊᕍ ᕆᕑᕆᓓᒃᕍᕊ ᐃᖅᐳᐱᕊᒍᕌᕊᕊ ᓂᕌᕑᕊ ᓇᓇᕆᕌᕑᕊᓯᕊᕊᕊᕊᓃ ᕍᕌᕍᕑᕑᕊᕍ ᑕᕍᕑᕌᕊ ᖄᕊᓂᕆᕊᕊᓚᕍᕊ. ᓂᓇ ᓇᕊᕍᕊᕍᕊ ᐅᕍᕍᕌᕈ ᐊᕊᕆᕊᖅᐳᑎᕊᐊᕌᕈᒃ.

ᐅᑐᕊ ᑐᕊᕊᐊᕊᕊ ᐱᕊᕆᕆᕆᕌᕊᕑᕊᕊᕑᕍᕑᕊ. ᓂᓓᕊ ᐃᖅᐳᐱᕊᕍᐳᕍᕍᕈᕊ. ᕍᕊ ᐱᐳᕊᕍᕆᕊᕌᕍᕊ ᐿᕊᕍᕍᖅᕆᕊᒍ. ᓚᓂᕊ ᑐᕊᕌᕆᕆᕍᕍᕈᕊᕊ. ᕑᕆᕝᕌᕆᕊ ᑐᕊᑐᕆᕍᕊ ᐊᕌᕍᕊ ᓚᓂ ᐊᕊᕌᕍᕆᕊᐿᕍᕈᕊᕊ. ᓇᓂ ᐿᕊᕍᐱᕌᕊᕊᕑᐿᕑ ᕍᕊ ᐱᕊᕌᕍᓂᕊᕊᕊᒍ. ᑲᓇᕋᓓᕊ ᐱᕊᕍᕍᕊᕊᕊ ᐊᕌᕍᕑ ᐅᐊᕋᕌᕑᕊ ᐃᐿᕌᕊᕆᕑᕊᕑᐊᕑᕑᕑᕊᒍᕊ. ᕍᕑᕍᕆᕊᕑᕑᕆᕊᒃ ᑕᕑᕑᕊᕊ ᐊᕍᓂ ᑕᐊᕍᕌᕑᕊ ᕍᕌᕑᕑᕊᐊᕊᐳᕍᕑᕍᕑᕍᕍᕈᕊ.

ᐊᑎᖅᖃᑎᑕᐅᖖᒥᑦᑐᖅ

ᐱᐊᕆ ᓇᖕᒪᓕᒃ, ᒍᓀᑦ 7

ᒃᐊᑎᓗ ᐊᖑᓇᓱᒡᕆᐊᖅᐳᔪᒃ. ᐅᑭᖅ ᖅᐅᐊᑦᖖᑐᖅᑐᖅ, ᖅᓱᖕᑦᕋᑎᓗ, ᐅᖅᕐᐃᖅᓄᑦ. ᙶᕐᓌ ᑐᓂᑦᑐᒍ. ᐊᑕᐅᒦᕐᑲ ᙶᕐᓌ ᐅᖅᖅᑲᖅᖃᑐᐁᓈᓘᒒᕐᒥ. ᐅᑎᑎᐊᕋᔪᐊᕋᑦᑲ ᐅᖅᕐᐃᖅᓄᑦ.

ᑖᒪ ᐊᕐᑲᕋᑦᑲ, ᑐᐱᖕᔪᑦ ᑕᖅᐃᖅᕐᕆᓄᐊᕋᑦᑲ ᑖᑕᓄᐊ. ᐃᑲᕐᖅᑕᐅᐊᕋᕐᕐᒪᓐᓄ ᑎᑭᑐᖅᖅᓂᓂᖅᖅᐸᑦᑕ. ᒥᖅᒍᐃᖅᕐᒉᐅᖅᑐᓄ ᑕᑯᕆᐊᕐᑉᓕᒐᖅᖅᓄᔪᒃ ᓇᕋᖅᕐᑎᓂᓴᒥᖅ. ᖅᐃᖅᑐᒍᕆᐊᕋᑦᑲ ᐃᓄᔅᒧᖕᔿᒥᖝ ᑕᑦᐊᑐᒍ.

ᐃᖕᒠᕐᕐᕆᖕ ᑖᑕᓄ ᐃᓗᐊᖕᒉ ᓇᓄᕐᔿᒍ. ᐃᖕᒡᕐᒺᐊᖅ ᖅᑉᒥᖑᓇᕐᑎᖣ. ᑖᒐᓐᑎ Ć・ᓇ ᓇᓴᖑᖅᑕᕐᑐ ᐱᓆᖏᖃᑎ. ᑕᑵᑐᓴᒉᑦ ᐃᓀᒉᐊᔪᒍ. ᑖᒪᓇ ᑐᐱᔔᐊᑲᑎᓴᖣ ᙶᑐᓳᖕᑦ ᐊᕘᓗ ᐃᖕᒡᕐᖑᑦ ᐊᒋᖅᖇᖅᖏᑐᓄ. ᙶᑕᖖᐊᓐᖣᓄᖃ ᓲᖅ ᐊᓵᒉᑎᑕᖖᐊᕐᖅᖏᑦ. ᓲᖃᑐᖅᖏᑎ ᖅᐅᕐᒺᖅᐃᕐᕐᕆᖅᖏᑐᑎ. ᖅᐅᕐᒺᖅ ᕙᖅᕐᕆᕋᔐᓐᔿᑐᑎ. ᓲᖃᑳᖕᐊᕐᕐᕆᕕᐊᖅᑐᓄ. ᓲᓇᖉᓇᑎᖕᖃᕐᖣ ᓲᖃᑐᐊᖅ ᙶᖅᔿᕐᐊᕐ ᙶᖅᐅᑎᐊᕐᖅᖏᑐᓄ. ᓲᖃᖕᔿᐅᑎᓐᖅ ᐅᓯᑦᕏᐅᔪᑦ ᐃᓄᔅᒉᓯᖏᓄᑦ ᐃᖕᒡᕐᒺᓐᖃᖅ ᐅᑎᖕᑎᓕᕐᑎᖖᒍ. ᒪᒋᐊᓇᕐᖅᐊᓐᖣ ᐊᕐᖅᖏᓄᑎ. ᐅᑎᖅᖅᑦ ᑐᐊᖅᖇᓄᓄᑦ ᖅᐅᕐᒺᑦᓯᓕᕋᐅᖅ ᓄᖅᖕᒪᖅᑎ. ᒃᐊᑕ ᐊᕘᓗ ᐅᕉᔾ ᐱᑐᖅᖅᓐᖅ ᑎᓕᒃᑦᖕᒺᓇᒥᖖᖄᕐᕇᓆᔐᑦ ᐃᖕᒡᕐᒺᓆᓂᑦ ᑖᒪᖝᒉᑐᖅᖅ.

Untitled
Barry Nangmalik, Grade 7

Jordy and I went out hunting. When we passed White Rock, Jordy got out of gas. I gave him gas. I had only one gallon left. When we were going back we ran out of gas.

Since we were stuck, we decided to put up the tent and relax. Hopefully someone would come by and help us. After relaxing we decided to explore. When we went up the hill we saw an old grave. There was a cup on the old grave. We left all our cups. So we took the old cup we found. I took it to a little lake and cleaned it out. So we took the cup to the tent and made tea and shared the cup.

After we had tea the wind started to change. It started to rain and lightning. The lightning was so bright and shiny. The heavy rain made the tent wet. We couldn't get to sleep from the rain and the lightning. We put on raincoats and ran to the old grave and put the old cup back. We apologized to the spirits. When we went to the tent the lightning stopped. The next day rangers found us. Jordy and I never stole old stuff from old graves anymore.

ᐊᕐᕕᐊᑦ	Arviat
ᑎᑭᕋᕐᔪᐊᖅ	Whale Cove
ᑲᖕᒋᖅᖠᓂᖅ	Rankin Inlet
ᑭᙵᓗᐊᑦ	Cape Dorset
ᐃᖃᓗᐃᑦ	Iqaluit
ᐸᖕᓂᖅᑑ	Pangnirtung
ᓇᓂᓯᕕᒃ	Nanisivik
ᒥᑦᑎᒪᑕᓕᒃ	Pond Inlet
ᐃᒃᐱᐊᕐᔪᒃ	Arctic Bay
ᖃᐅᓱᐃᑦᑐᖅ	Resolute Bay
ᐊᐅᔪᐃᑦᑐᖅ	Grise Fiord

ᑲᖕᒋᖅᑐᓂᖅ
ᑕᐅ ᐅᓴᒃ ᐃᓕᓐᓂᐊᕐᕕᒃ

Rankin Inlet
Leo Ussak School

ᓄᓇᓕᐹᕐᓱᖅᑐᖅ ᑲᖕᒋᖅᑐᓂᖅ ᒪᔪᓕᖅᕸᐅᐱᖅ ᐊᒻᓗ ᓇᖕᒥᓂᖅ ᐱᓕᕆᐊᖅᓱᖅᑐᖅ ᐱᓕᕆᖕᐊᐅᑕᖕ ᑭᕙᓪᓕᕐᒥ. ᑕᐃᑯᓂ ᐊᕕᒃᑐᖅᓯᒪᐅᕝᒥ ᐃᓄᒋᐊᕐᓂᕐᐸᐅᕐᓱᖅ ᐃᓄᖅᓱᖅᑐᖅ, 500- ᓂᑯ ᐊᒻᓗ ᐊᖅᑯᒃᓴᐅᑕᖕᓇᓂ. ᑲᖕᒋᖅᑐᓂᖅ ᐃᕐᑕᖕᔭᐅᕐᓯᓚᕐᖅ ᓴᓇᖕᒍᐊᕐᐸᐅᑕᕐᓂᖕᓚᕐ ᓚᖕᕐᓂᖕ, ᐊᒻᓗ ᐊᖕᒋᖕᓇᔭᐅᖕᓚᖕᓇ ᐃᓄᖕᔭᖕ ᓯᕐᓚᕐᖕᓚᖕᓚᖕ ᓱᐊᖅᖕᖕᑎᐅᕐᔪᖕ NHL- ᑰᖕᓄᖕ, ᔮᐊᑕᖕ ᑑᑑ. ᓄᓇᐅᖕ ᑕᐅᑐᖕᖄ ᖃᓄᐃᖕᓂᖕᖄ ᐊᕐᕈᖕᖕᑎᕐᑐᖅ, ᐃᑎᖕᓗᔭᖕ ᓇᖅᖕᔭᐅᖕᓗᓂ, ᐊᕐᕈᖕᖕᑎᐅᑕᖕᓗ ᐅᔭᖅᖃᕐᖃᐅᖅᓱᖕᓄᓂ, ᐊᐅᕐᖕᑯᖕᓗ ᓄᓇᖃᕐᔪᖕᖃᐅᖅᓱᖕᓄᓂ ᐱᕐᓱᖅᑐᖕᓂᖕᓗ. ᐊᐅᕐᔭᒥ ᐃᖕᑰᖕᖕᑎᕐᑰᖕᑰ ᐅᖅᑯᔮᕐᖃᖕᓄᖕᓂᖅᑐᖅ 20°C-ᒥᖕ. ᐅᐱᖕᖕᖃ ᐊᐅᔭᒥᖕᓗ, ᓯᖕᖕᑑᖕᖃᖅᑐᖅ ᐊᒻᓗ ᑕᖕᓯᕐᕿᖕᓂᖕᓂ, ᐅᐱᐅᒥᖕᓗ, ᐱᖕᔾᑯᖕᓄᖕᓗ, ᐊᒻᓚ ᐊᓇᑎᑰᖕᓂᖕᓗ, ᐊᒻᓚ ᑕᖕᔾᕐᔾᖕᓂᖕᓗ.

The modern community of Rankin Inlet is the governmental and business hub for Kivalliq. This largest hamlet of the region has a population of 2,500 and a high volume of commercial traffic. Rankin is known for its ceramic arts, and for being the hometown of the first Inuk athlete to play professional hockey in the NHL, Jordin Tootoo. The topography is varied, with flat areas, intricate rock formations, and tundra valleys that fill with small wildflowers in the summer. During these months, temperatures can reach a warm 20°C. During the spring and fall months, patches of rain or fog are common, while in the winter, high winds, blizzards, and ice fogs occur frequently.

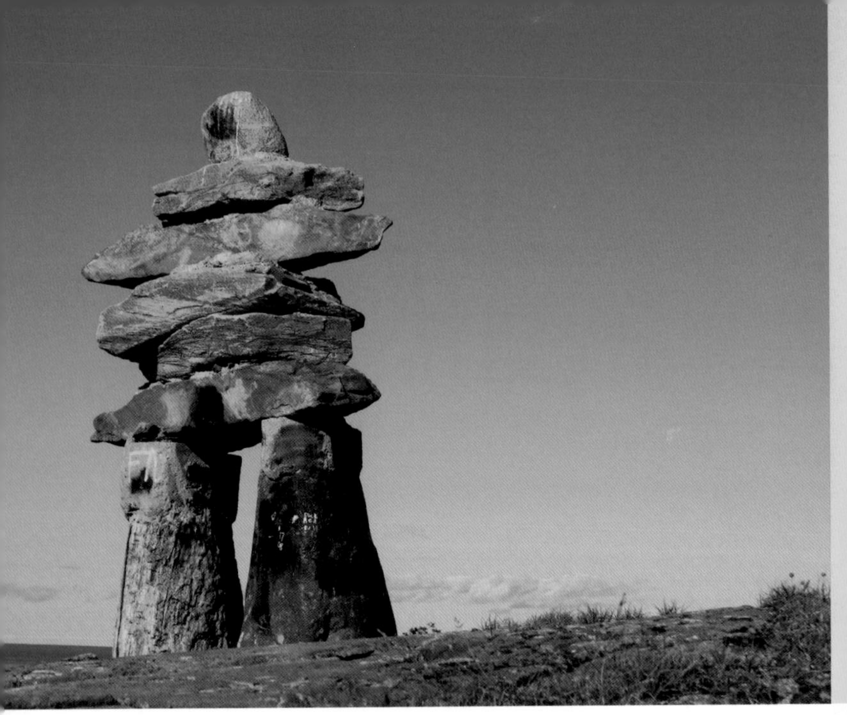

The Wolf That Howled at the Northern Lights

Leslie Dean, Age 10

Once there lived a little wolf. One day the wolf got lost in a big storm. The next day he found a shelter. That night there were the northern lights, the wolf didn't know what they were. He said "Who are you?" A great polar bear answered, "I am the great Northern Lights, sing for me and I will dance." The wolf said, "How do I sing?"

"With your mouth," the polar bear said.

So the wolf howled and howled but it was not singing, the bear didn't like it. The bear grew bigger and bigger and he grabbed the wolf to the northern lights and they danced together.

ᐊᒪᕈᖅ ᒥᐊᒡᒎᖅᑐᕕᓂᖅ ᐊᖅᓴᕐᓂᓗᑦ

ᓕᐊᔅᓕ ᑏᓐ, 10-ᓂᒃ ᐅᑭᐅᓕᒃ

ᑕᐃᒪᒎᖅ ᐊᒪᕈᑯᓗᖅᑲᓚᐅᖅᑐᖅ. ᐅᑦᓗᑉ ᐃᓚᖓᓐᓂ ᐊᒪᕈᖅ ᐱᖅᑐᒥ ᐊᓯᐅᑦᓗᓂ. ᐅᑦᓗ ᑐᒡᓕᐊᓂ ᐃᓂᒋᔪᓐᓇᖅᑕᒥᓂᒃ ᓇᐃᐱᑦᓯᑦᓗᓂ. ᐅᓐᓄᐊᒃᑯᑦ ᐊᖅᓴᕐᓂᖅᑲᐅᑦᑕᕐᒪᑦ, ᐊᒪᕈᖅ ᖃᐅᔨᒪᓇᓂ ᓱᓇᐅᖕᒪᖔᑕ. ᐅᖅᑲᐅᑎᑦᓗᓂᒋᑦ, "ᑭᓇᐅᕕᓯ?" ᓇᓄᕐᔪᐊᕌᓗᒃ ᑭᐅᑦᓗᓂ, "ᐊᖅᓴᕐᓂᐊᓘᔪᖓ, ᐅᕙᓐᓄᑦ ᐃᒻᖏᓇᑦ ᐊᒻᒪ ᒧᒥᕐᓂᐊᖅᐳᖓ." ᐊᒪᕈᖅ ᑭᐅᑦᓗᓂ, "ᖃᓄᕐᓕ ᐃᒻᖏᓚᖓᕗᖓ?"

"ᖃᓃᑦ ᐊᑐᕐᓗᒍ," ᓇᓄᖅ ᑭᐅᑦᓗᓂ.

ᐊᒪᕈᖅ ᒥᐊᒡᒎᔪᖕᒪᑦ ᒥᐊᒡᒎᙱᓐᓇᓚᖅᑐᓂ ᑭᓯᐊᓂᓚ ᐃᒻᖏᕐᓂᐅᙱᒪᑦ, ᓇᓅᑉ ᐊᓚᐊᓇᐃᒋᓇᓂᐅᒃ. ᓇᓄᖅ ᐊᖏᒡᓚᕙᓪᓚᐊᑦᑐᓂ ᐊᖏᒡᓚᒃᑲᓐᓂᖅᑐᓂ ᐊᒻᒪᓗ ᐊᒪᕈᖅ ᐃᒋᑦᓯᓂᐅᒃ ᐊᖅᓴᕐᓂᓄᑦ ᒧᒥᖅᑲᑎᒋᓚᖅᑐᓂᐅᒃ.

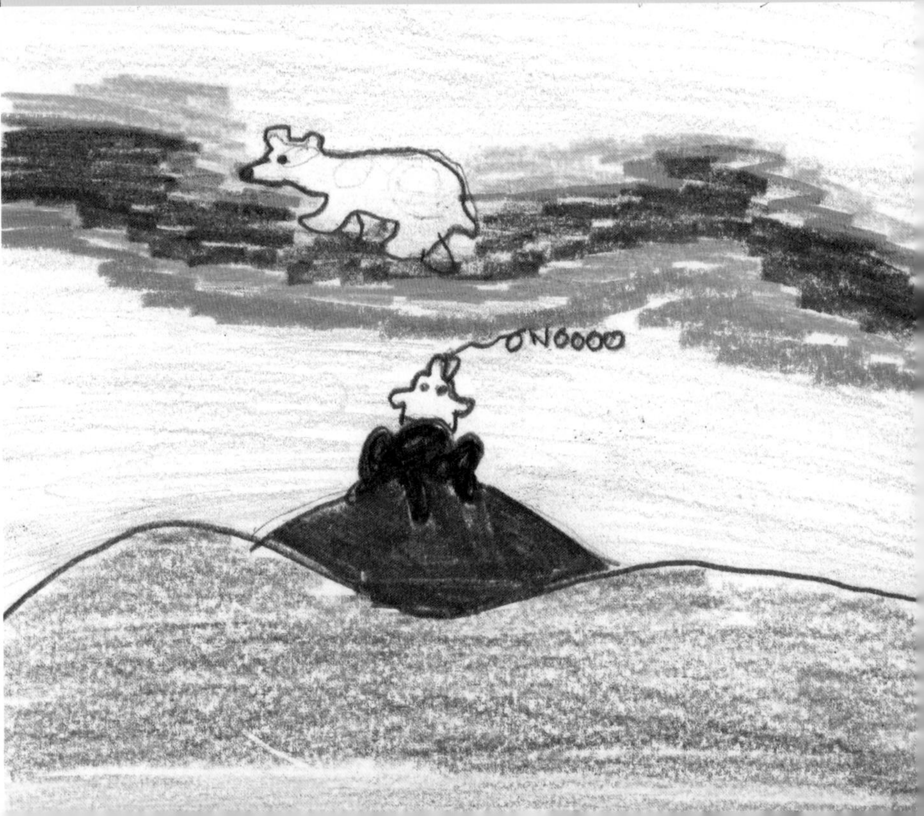

ᓇᓄᖅ ᑲᒃᑐᖅ

ᔭᒻᔅ ᑳᓄᓕ, 10-ᓂᒃ ᐅᑭᐅᓕᒃ

ᐅᑉᓗᖅ ᐃᓇᖕᒥᓂ ᓇᑎᕐᖅᕿᐅᕆᐊᖃᐅᑎᖅᑐᒍᑦ. ᓇᔪᕐᒥᒐᓗ
ᑕᒃᓗᒍᖅᑐᒍᑦ ᑭᓱᐊᓴ ᐱᐊᕋᐅᑉᓗᓂ. ᑐᓄᖕᒍᑦ ᕿᕕᐊᕿᒐᓗ
ᓇᓄᒥᒃ ᑕᑲᓗᖕᒐᓗ. ᐅᖃᖅᖁᖕᒐᓗ, "ᐊᑖᑕᒃ, ᑕᐃᑲ ᓇᓄᖅ
ᓇᑎᕐᔭᕐᒥᒃ ᓂᕐᑐᖅᒃ." ᐅᓇᑎᓐᓂᒃ ᐱᓇᓯᕐᕕᐊᕐᔪᐊᒐᕆ,
ᑭᓱᐊᓴ ᓯᖕᒃᐃᓗᖅᑐᖅᑐᓂ. ᐊᖕᕐᕿᓗᑕ ᐊᖁᓇ
ᐅᓇᖅᑲᐅᓐᓗᒍ ᑕᑯᓚᖅᑖᖕᖅ. ᐅᓇᐅᔪᒍᖕᒐᑦ
ᐊᒃᓗ ᕆᓀ ᐱᓯᖁᐅᓐᓂᖅᑐᓂ. ᐅᑉᓗᐊᒐ ᐃᓇᖕᒃᑯᓂ
ᐱᖕᒃᔭᖅᑐᒍᑦ ᕈᓐᒥ ᕈᒻᒥ ᐊᒃᓗ ᓇᓄᖅ ᑕᑲᖕᖄᓯᓄᖕᒐᑐᒍ
ᕿᕕᐊᕐᔭᒐ ᐊᖕᕐᕿᓐᖕᒐᓄᖕᑦ. ᓇᓄᖅ ᕆᓀ ᐊᐃᐊᖔᓇᐅᕐᔪᒐ
ᓂᓇᑐᖅᕝᒪᕆᓐᓂᑦ ᓇᔪᕐᒥᒃ. ᓂᐅᑕ ᐅᕆᖅᑲᓂ ᐊᐅᓇᖅᑕ
ᓇᐱᖕᖅᑐᓂ. ᐱᖕᒃᓅᕈᕐᔭ ᐊᑖᑕᓪᒪᑦ ᕿᒃᐅᕆᑲᖕᕆᐊᖅᑐᒍ

ᓇᓄᖅᑦ ᐱᔭᐅᓇᖕᖅᓄᖅᓯᒄᖕᒃᓇ. ᐊᑖᑕᖕᒃᓇ ᐅᓂᑯᖕᒐ
ᕿᕈᐅᒥᕆᓂᒃ ᐊᐃᐊᕐᔭᖕᒐ. ᕿᕈᐅᒥᓂᖕᒃ ᑕᒃᕙᐅᒃᑲᖅᑐᖅ
30 30-ᓂᖕᖅᒃᑕᐅᓐᖕᒍᓂ. ᓇᓄᕐᒃ ᑐᓅᑎᕐᖕᒐᐅᖅᑐᖕᒃ
ᐅᑉᓗᐅᖀᖕᒃ ᓂᐅᑐ ᓯᖕᖖᒃᓂᓐᒃᓄᐅᑖᖅ. ᐊᑖᑕᖕᒐ
ᕿᕈᐊᒄᖕᓅᐊᒐᕆ ᕈᓇᐅᐳᒃᑐᓐᒃᓅᖕᒐ ᐊᒃᓗ ᐃᓇᖖᒐᑦ
ᑲᒃᐱᐊᕐᔫᐊᖕᓂᖕᓅᖕᒐᓕᖕᒃ. ᓇᓄᖅ ᐱᓯᐅᕐᕿᖖᒃᖀ ᕿᐳᒃᕆᓐᓂ
ᐊᑕᒄᐅᓪᒄᖕᒃᖕᑐᒃᑦ.

The Hungry Bear
James Connelly, Age 10

One day we were going seal hunting. We saw a seal but it was a baby seal. I looked back and saw a polar bear. I said, "Dad, look there is a polar bear eating the baby seal." The polar bear tried to get us, but it was too slow. We went back home and told the story to my mother. Now it was night and the weather was very bad. The next day my friends and I were playing near the ice and we saw the polar bear again and then ran up to our house. The polar bear was still full of blood by the seal meat.

I broke my leg by a rock. My friends went to go tell my dad that the polar bear was trying to get me. My dad ran and got his gun. The gun was called 30 30. He aimed at the polar bear but he missed and the polar bear bit the same leg. My dad shot again and then ran out of bullets. I got real mad because my dad ran out of bullets and my friends were very scared. So I started going after the polar bear and the polar bear ran like a little lemming.

ᐊᖅᓴᖅᓃᑦ

ᐃᐅᔩᓐ ᖃᐸᓗᐃᑦᑐᖅ, 07-ᓂᒃ ᐅᑭᐅᓕᒃ

ᐅᓐᓄᐊᒥ ᑕᑯᕗᖓ ᐊᖅᓴᖅᓂᓂᒃ. ᖅᑭᒥᖅᓱᑦᑎᐊᓕᖅᑭᑦ ᐊᑖᑕᓯᐊᕋ ᐊᒻᒪᓗ ᐊᒃᑲᒐ ᑕᑯᓇᓱᒋᑦᑐᒋᑦ ᑕᒃᐱᑲᓂ ᓯᓚᒥ. ᐊᒃᑲᒪ ᐅᖅᑲᐅᑎᑦᑐᓂᖓ, “ᓱᖅ ᐅᕙᓐᓄᑦ ᐃᔨᒥᕙᑦ?” ᐊᑖᑕᒪᓗ ᐊᓈᓇᓯᐊᖓ ᐊᑖᑕᓯᐊᖓᓗ ᑕᑯᒋᑦᑐᒋᑦ. ᖅᑯᕕᐊᓚᐅᕋᓗᐊᖅᖢᖓ ᐃᓚᒃᑲ ᑕᑯᒐᒃᑭᑦ, ᖅᑭᐊᓕᖅᖢᖓ ᑭᖕᒍᓂᐊᒍᑦ. ᑭᓯᐊᓂᓕ ᖅᑯᕕᐊᓱᓚᐅᖅᑐᖓ ᓱᓕ ᐅᕙᓃᒻᒪᑕ. ᐊᖕᒋᖅᕋᑦᑎᓐᓄᐊᕋᒪ ᐊᓈᓇᓐᓄᑦᑐ ᐊᑖᑕᓐᓄᑦᓕᑐ ᐊᐱᕆᔪᐅᑦᑐᖓ ᐃᒪᓐᓇ, “ᓱᖅ ᖅᑭᐊᕕᒃ?”

ᐅᖅᑲᐅᑎᑦᑐᒥᒃ, “ᐃᓛᒃ ᐊᓈᓇᓯᐊᕋ ᐊᑖᑕᓯᐊᕋᓗ ᐅᖕᒐᒥᒐᓗᐊᖅᑭᑦ.”

ᑕᐃᑲᓂ ᐅᓐᓄᖕᒪᑦ ᓯᓂᒃᑎᑦᑐᖓ ᓯᓐᓇᒃᑐᖅᐳᖓ ᐊᖅᓴᖅᓂᓂᒃ. ᑐᐸᒃᑲᒪ ᐊᓈᓇ ᐅᖅᑲᐅᑎᑦᑐᒍ, “ᐊᓈᓇᒃ, ᐱᐅᔪᒥᒃ ᓯᓐᓇᒃᑐᖅᑲᐅᔪᖓ. ᐊᖅᓴᖅᓂᓂᒃ.”

ᓇᔭᒐ ᐊᐱᕆᑦᑐᓂ, “ᖃᓄᐃᖅᑲᐅᓐᓂᖅᑭᑦ ᓯᓐᓇᑦᑑᒪᑎᑦᑐᑎᑦ? ᖃᐅᔨᒪᓚᐅᖅᓂᖏᑦᑐᖓ ᕼᐋᓗᐃᖑᓚᐅᖅᓂᖓᓂᒃ ᐅᓐᓄᐊᓂ.

The Northern Lights

Eugene Kabluitok, Age 7

One night I saw the northern lights. When I looked carefully I thought I saw my grandpa and my uncle in the sky. My uncle said, “Why are you looking at me?” I also saw my dad’s grandpa and grandma. I was so happy to see my family, then I cried sadly when I saw them. But it also made me feel happy that they were still with me. When I went back into my house my mom and dad asked me, “Why are you crying?”

I said, “Because I miss my grandparents.”

That night when I was sleeping I had a dream about the northern lights. When I woke up I told my Mom, “Mom, I had a nice dream. It was about the northern lights.”

My sister said, “What happened in your dream?” I didn’t know it was Hallowe’en night.

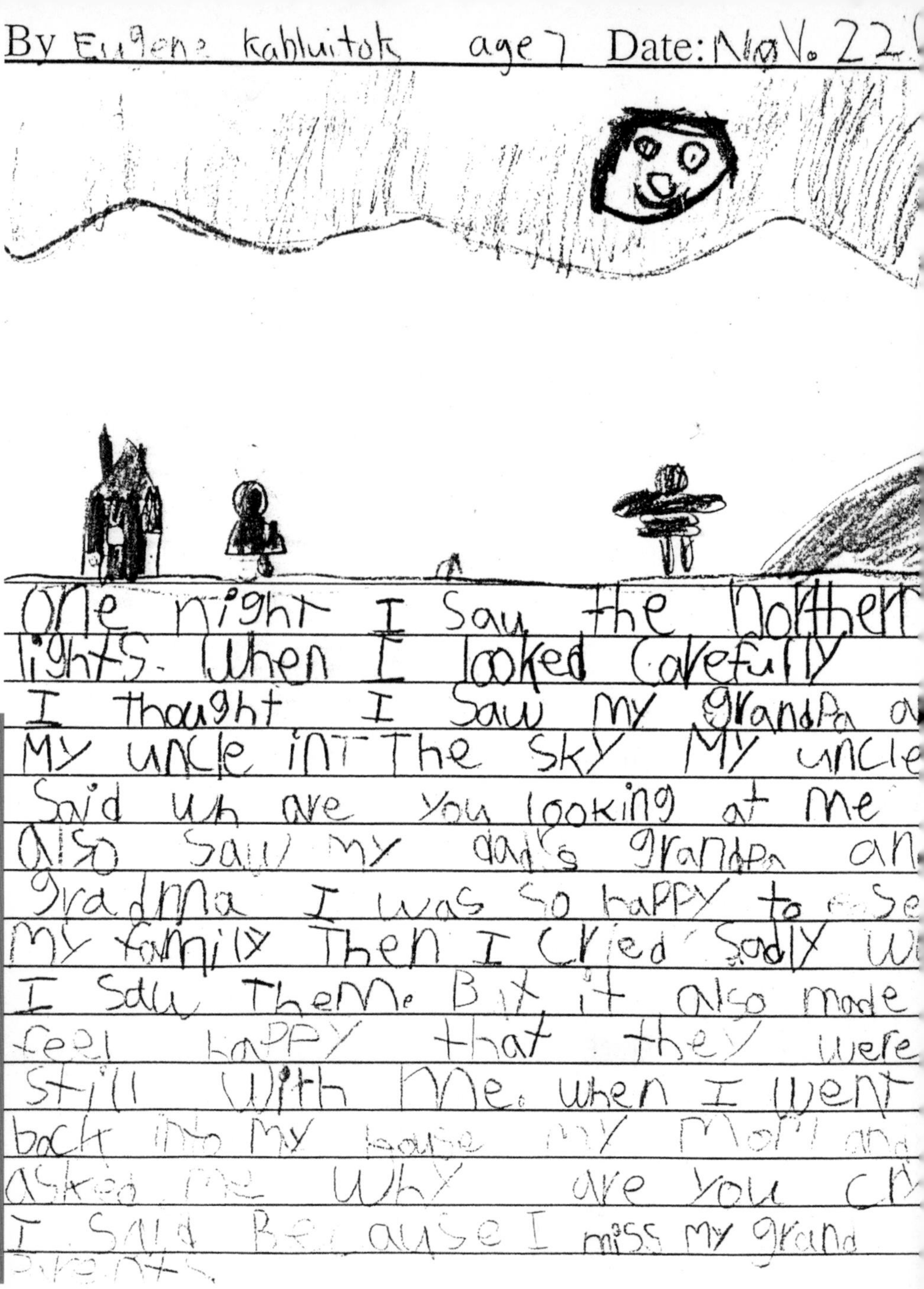

29

⊲ˢ᠍ᑕ⊲ᑦ	Arviat
∩ᑭᖅˢᒉ⊲ᖅ	Whale Cove
ᑲᐋ∩ᖅᑊᐸᔪᖅ	Rankin Inlet
ᑭᐴᖕᒪᐃᑦ	Cape Dorset
ᐃᖅᒍᐃᑦ	Iqaluit
ᐸᖕᓂᖅᒍ	Pangnirtung
ᓇᓂᓯᕕᒃ	Nanisivik
ᒥᑦ∩ᒪᑕᓯᒃ	Pond Inlet
ᐃᒃᐱᐊᖅᔪᒃ	Arctic Bay
ᖃᐅᓯᐅᐃᑕᑐᖅ	Resolute Bay
⊲ᐅᔅᐃᑕᑐᖅ	Grise Fiord

ᑭᖕᒥᐅᑦ
ᐱᑕ ᐱᓯᐅᓖᐊᒃ
ᐃᓕᓐᓂᐊᕐᕕᖕᓕ

Cape Dorset
Peter Pitseolak
School

ᑭᖕᒥᐅᑦ, ᑕᐃᑯᖓ ᑭᖕᒥᐅᑦ ᖅᑭᖅᑲᖕᓗᖓᑦᑐᖅ ᔭᑯᖏᑉ ᖃᓂᒋᔭᖓᑦᑐᖅ, ᖃᐅᔪᓕᕐᐸᑦᑐᓂᒐ ᔭᐸᓪᔭᐊᑲᓕᒥ ᓴᐅᐱᖕᑎᖃᐅᑦᓂᖁᓄᑦ ᐊᒡᓴᓐᖅ ᐱᔪᕐᓇᕐᔪᐊᖅᑐᓐᖅ ᐊᒡᓗ ᑕᑯᕝᕐᓯᑎᐊᕐᖃᓐᐊᕐᑎᓐᖅ. ᐃᓄᐃᑦ ᐊᒡᔫᑎᑎᕐᔪᑦ ᐃᓗᐊᓇ 1,300-ᓂᖅ ᐊᒡᓗ ᓄᓇᖅᑯᒃ ᒪᓇᕿᕐᔪᑦᓯᓄ, ᐳᖅᑐᕐᔪᑐᓂᖁ ᐱᖔᖕᑲᖅᖅᓂᖁ. ᔭᓂᓄᔪᖅᑐᖅ ᔭᖅᖄᓂᓂᓯᔪᕐᔪᖑᓂᖁ, ᐃᓇᖕᓂᔪᑦ ᑕᑯᕕᔪᑎᖅᔪᖑᓂᖁ, ᔭᕆᔾᔪᖅᔪᖅᖅᖑᓂᖁᓗ. ᐅᑭᐅᒥ, ᐃᖅᖀᓇᑕᒐᖕᓴᑦᓄᖅᑎᑭᖑᓖᓐᖑᑦ -40°C.

ᐱᑕ ᐱᓯᐅᓖᐊᖕᒐᖅ ᐃᓕᓐᓂᐊᕐᕕᖕᓐᖅ ᐊᑎᖕᖅᖕᑎᖅᐅᔪᖅᔪᖅ ᐃᓐᑕᑭᓕᑦᔪᖁᓕᔾᑭᖕᒪᖑ ᑭᖕᒥᓓ ᐊᔾᔭᑕᐅᓐᔭᐅᑕᐅᖅᖑᒐᑳᖑᒐ, ᓴᓇᖕᐩᐊᖑᔪᖕᑎᖅᒪᖕᓆᖑᓂᖁᓄᖁᓯᖑᓂᖁᓯ, ᐊᒡᓗ ᔾᕺᖕᓂᖕᒐᖕᒐᖁ ᐅᓂᖕᑲᕐᖃᕐᐱᖕᑕᕐᖅᑐᔾᖁᓐᖅ. ᐃᓇᔭᖕᖁᖕᒐᖁᒐᖕᒐᖁ ᐅᓂᖕᑲᕐᖁᓄᓴᔭᕐᓇᖕᖑ ᐊᒡᓗ ᑲᖕᖁᖕᖃᖁᖅᔭᖕᑕᖑᑕᖁᕺᒐᖁᔾ ᐱᓕᔾᑭᐅᕐᔪᑦ ᐊᔾᔭᑕᐅᑕᖁᖕᖅᖑᖕᖁᖑᕺᖁ ᐅᖅᖃᓕᔪᖕᓕᒐᖕᕺᑐᖁ ᐊᖕᑕᖕᓄᖕᒐᖕᖑ ᖃᖕᓗᔾᖕᕺᖑᖁ People From Our Side ᐊᒡᔾᒐᕐᓄᖅᖃᕐᕺᑕᕐᑕᕐᑐᖕᖑ ᑎᖕᑎᔭᖕᖁᖕᖁᓐᒐ ᐃᖁᕺᖁᔾᖑᔾᖕᖂᖁᓕᓐᖑᖅᖅᖕᖁᑐᖕᖂᖁᑐᒐᖅ.

Cape Dorset, located on Dorset Island adjacent to Foxe Peninsula, is world-renowned for its artwork and community of visual artists. With a population of 1,300, Cape Dorset is a vibrant community situated on fairly flat terrain, with some gentle hills. The climate is generally mild and sunny, although sometimes in the fall it can be foggy, with heavy rains. In the winter, the temperature can drop to –40°C.

Peter Pitseolak School is named after an acclaimed Cape Dorset photographer, artist, sculptor, and historian. A biography and collection of Pitseolak's photographs named *People From Our Side* was published posthumously.

ᐱᖅᑐᐃᑦ

ᑯᕕ L.

ᐱᖅᑐᐃᑦ ᖁᕕᐊᓇᖅᑐᑦ, ᐊᒻᒪᓗ ᐃᒃᐱᐊᖅᑕᐅᓐᖏᑦ. ᖅᑲᑕᑦᔭᖅᓯᐊᒃᑯᑦ ᓯᑭᑑᒃᑯᕕᐅᑦ ᓄᐊᒃᑖᒃᑑᑦᒍᓄᑦ ᓴᑉᑕᑦ ᑕᑯᒃᑲᐃᐳᓇᒪᖕᒥᑎᑎᐊᖅᑐᖅ. ᐊᒻᒪᓗ ᒪᖅᐃᓇᖅᑳᑦᑕᕆᔭ ᐱᖅᖅᓱᑎᑦᒍ! ᐃᓇᖕᓂᑦ ᐃᓄᐃᑦ ᐊᔪᐃᔪᒫᔪ ᐱᖅᖅᓱᑎᑦᒍ. ᑕᐃᑯᓇ ᓇᖅᐸᓇᖅᑐ ᐅᒡᓗᒥ ᐊᑕᐅᓯᒐᒥ ᐃᑲᖅᖅᒐᒥ ᐊᑕᐅᓯᒐᒍᓄᑦ. ᐱᖅᖅᔭᖅᖱᖅᕝᑳ ᓄᖅᑐᐊᒍᒍ ᐱᔅᑯᓄᑦ ᐱᓕᖅᖅᓱᑦᒍ. ᐸᖅᓇᖅᑐᒍᒍ ᐃᖕᓕᖕᒐᐱᑎᔭ ᐱᓕᖅᔪᖕᑦ ᐊᒻᒪᓗ ᐊᖕᓕᖕᒐᑎᑦᒍᓄᑦ.

Blizzards

Kov M.

Blizzards are fun, and it is not cold. And if you ride on a Ski-Doo or truck you can barely see. And don't go hunting when there is a blizzard! Some people were lost because of a blizzard. You should stay about a day or an hour. After the blizzard's past you should pack. After you pack start your machine and go home.

Kudlu Kellypalik, Age 12, Grade 7
ᑯᑦᓗ ᖅᐱᓐᖅᐸᓐᑉ, 12-ᓂᖅ ᐅᑭᐅᖅ, ᒍᕿᑦ 7

True Story

Ning Parr, Age 14

Once upon a time there was a man named Kov T. who was lost outland near Cape Dorset. His Ski-Doo wasn't working. He was making small holes to make an iglu, but he didn't have a knife. He was using his hands and feet. He had a bed, it was a dried caribou skin and he had his clothes for a blanket, even if they were wet. When he slept, he was so cold. When he got warmer he woke up and put his clothes on. He was walking around, and he tried to stand up his qamutiiks to keep warm. He took his rifle to look for a fox or anything to eat. But he went back to his iglu. At night he went to sleep. Next day he had hot water, because he didn't have tea bags. A few hours later, he heard a sound like a Ski-Doo. It was Nuna. Kov didn't believe it was Nuna. Then they both went to Kov's outpost camp. The next day they went to Cape Dorset, then Kov was talking on the radio, thanking the community.

ᐅᓂᒃᑲᖅ ᓲᓚᐊᖅ

ᓂᕐ ᐸ, 14-ᓂᒃ ᐅᑭᐅᓕᒃ

ᑕᐃᑦᓱᒪᓂᔫᖅ ᐃᓄᖃᖅᑕᐅᖅᑑᖅ ᐊᑎᓕᒃ ᒃᐅᐊ ᐱᑕ.-ᒥᒃ ᐊᓯᐅᐸᑕᐅᖅᑑᒥᒃ, ᑭᖕᒥᐃᑦ ᖃᓂᒋᔮᓂ. ᖃᒧᑎᐅᔪᖕ ᐊᕐᑖᓯᐊᖕᒪᑦ. ᐃᔨᓘᑕᐅᔭᕆᐊᖓᕐᒥ, ᐸᓇᖃᖅᓂᐊᖓᒥ, ᐊᐅᒪᒃ ᔭᓇᓯᖅᑑᖕ ᐳᑐᑕᐅᖅ ᔫᓂ ᒥᑭᑐᓂᒃ. ᐊᖕᓂ ᐃᔨᓯᓇᔪ ᐊᑑᖅᑑᓂᒃ. ᐃᔨᓕᖃᖕᓂᓇᒥ, ᐸᓂᖅᓯᒪᔨᕕᓂᒃ ᑐᒃᑐᐃᑦ ᐊᒥᐊᖕᓂᒃ ᐊᓕᓗ ᐊᖃᒋᖓᒥᒃ ᖃᐱᖃᖅᔫᓂ, ᖃᑭᐅᓱᖃᐊᖅᖅᐸᑕ. ᓱᓂᓴᐅᒪᒋ ᐃᑭᐸᖅᑐᑯᓖᑦᖃᖅᔫᓂ. ᐅᖃᒃᔨᓴᐅᒪᒋ ᐊᖃᓄᖅᖃᖅᐸᔫᓂ. ᐱᓯᕆᖃᐊᔫᓂ, ᐊᓖᓗ ᖃᒧᑎᓂ ᓇᕝᕝᓯᔾᓚᓇᔭᔫᓂᒃ ᐅᖃᐊᖃᖅᔾᓚᓇᔭᔫᓂᒃ. ᖁᐸᐅᐱᕐᔭᒋ ᑎᑎᓚᓇᐊᓱᓖᔾᑦᖀᒃ ᓲᓇᑐᐊᓇᓱᓖᔭ ᐱᓇᖅᖃᖅᔫᓂ. ᐃᔨᓘᒥᒃᑦ ᐅᑎᖅᖃᖅᔫᓂ. ᐅᐊᓄᖃᑦ ᓯᓄᖅᖃᖅᔫᓂ. ᐅᑦᔭᐊᑎ ᐃᒥᖃᕐᒥ ᐅᓇᖅᔫᒥ ᐃᒥᕆᖃᖅᔫᓂ ᐱᖃᖅᖓᒥ. ᐸᓕᓱᐊᒍᑦ ᐊᕿᓯᖅᖃᖅᔫᓂ ᑐᑕᖅᖃᖅᔫᓂ ᖃᒧᑕᐅᐅᖅᓯᐅᖅᔭᕆᒥ. ᓲᓇᐅᕝᕉᑕ ᓄᓇ. ᒃᐅᐊ ᓄᓇᑦᓴᖀᒡᓄᒃ ᑕᐃᒃᑯᖅᖃᑎᕋᔪᖃᑭᐅᓇᕐᓖ. ᖃᖅᔫᑦ ᑭᖕᒥᓄᒃ ᐊᐅᑦᓪᖃᖓᒃ, ᒃᐅᐊᓗ ᐂᑎᐅᑐᕐᖃᖅᔫᓂ, ᓄᐊᔾᑉᐆᓂᒃ ᖃᑯᓂᒪᕐᖃᖅᔫᓂ ᐃᐱᔪᖅᑐᖅᔭᔮᒃ.

ᐊᕐᕕᐊᑦ	Arviat
∩ᕇᕋᕝᑲᐊᕝ	Whale Cove
ᑲᖕᒋᕝᑭᖕᒥᕝ	Rankin Inlet
ᑭᖕᒥᓗᐊᑦ	Cape Dorset
ᐃᕐᑲᓗᐃᑦ	Iqaluit
ᐸᖕᓂᕐᑰ	Pangnirtung
ᓇᓂᓯᕕᒃ	Nanisivik
ᒥᑦᑎᒪᑕᓕᒃ	Pond Inlet
ᐃᒃᐱᐊᕐᔪᒃ	Arctic Bay
ᕃᐅᔨᐊᑦᑐᖅ	Resolute Bay
ᐊᐅᔪᐃᑦᑐᖅ	Grise Fiord

ᐃᖃᓗᐃᑦ
ᓇᑲᓱᒃ ᐃᓕᓐᓂᐊᕐᕕᖕᒐ

Iqaluit
Nakasuk School

ᐃᖃᓗᐃᑦ ᐊᖏᔪᖅᑲᑯᒡᑯᐊᐅᑎᖅ ᑐᐱᓚᐅᑎᖅ ᓄᓇᕗᒡᑎ, ᐊᒻᒪᓗ ᐃᓄᐃᓯᐊᓂᖅᑲᐸᒎᑎᓂᐅᑦ ᐊᒡᓯᓂᓗ ᐃᓄᖃᖅᑲᕐᑕᐊᑐᐊᒎ ᓄᓇᖓᒥᓯᓕᖅ, ᐊᒡᓯᓂᖕᕿᑕ ᐃᓄᐃᑦ ᐃᒪᖔ 7,250. ᐃᖃᓗᐃᑦ ᑐᐸᑦᕿᕐᕿᐅᕿᖅ ᒐᕐᕕᓐᓂᓗᒎᑦ, ᐊᑐᓯᖅᑐᓯᓂᓗᒎᑦ, ᐅᖃᓕᓐᓂᖅᑯᑦ ᓂᑎᑎᖅᑲᑯᒡᑯᐊᐅᓂᓗᒎᑦ, ᐊᒻᒪᓗ ᓇᖕᓯᓂᖅ ᐱᓕᕿᐊᖅᖕᓂᓗᒎᑦ. ᐃᖃᓗᐃᑦᑲᑐᖅ

ᐊᑐᓯᖅᕿᒡᕿᖅ ᐃᓕᖅᑯᒧᒡᓯᓗᒎᑦ ᐃᒐᒡᓯᓂᒐᖅ ᐅᑦᒎᒥ ᐊᑐᖅᑕᐅᑦᖅᑐᖅ. ᓄᓇᖕᓯ ᒪᓯᖅᑕᐃᕋᐱᐊᐅᓯᓂ ᐱᐅᔫᖅᑲᐅᑐᖅᖅ, ᓇᖅᑲᕿᑕᐅᖅᑯᓂ ᐊᒻᒪᓗ ᐅᔭᖅᑲᖅᑲᐅᖅᑲᓂ ᐳᖅᑐᑐᓂᖅ, ᐅᓯᓚᕿ ᐱᒥᓗ (ᑕᐃᒪᖔ ᐃᖃᓗᐃᑦ ᐊᑎᖅᑲᑕᕿᖅᑎᒎᔾ) ᑎᓇᐅᕋᒡᓕᑎ ᐅᓕᕐᑕᕿᖕᕿᑦ ᐱᓗᐊᓯᓂᖅᑲᐅᕐᕿᑦ ᑲᓇᑕᒡᒥᒎ. ᐊᕐᕼᑭᕿᐅᖔᖅᔾ ᑕᒡᑲᔅᐅᑦᑕᐅᑦᑕᑐᖅ ᐊᕐᔪᐊᕿᑦ ᐱᖅᖏᕐᒎᑦ. ᐊᐃᕙᕙᓗ, ᐅᑦᒎᑦ ᐃᖃᓗᖕᓂ ᑕᖅᑯᒎᓂᖅ ᓯᖅᐯᓯᕐᕼᓄᒎᓯᓂ ᐃᒪᖄᓐᒥ 16-ᓂ ᐃᑳᖅᑲᓂ ᐅᑦᓗᑐᖅᖔᓂᖅ, ᐃᓕᖅᓯᓂᓗ ᐃᒪᖄᓐᒥ 24-ᓂ ᐃᑳᖅᑲᓂ ᓯᖅᐸᓂᖅᖄᖃᐅᑐᖅᖔᓂ ᔾᓂ ᐊᑐᑐᖅᑲᖅᑎᓐᖄᑑ ᐊᒻᒪᓗ 4-ᓂ ᐃᑳᖅᑎᐊᖄᓇᖅᐹᓂ ᐅᑦᓗᒡᑯᖅᔾᓂ ᑎᒡᓯᐱᐅᑎᓯᖅᕙᖕᕿᑦ. ᑲᐟᓂᖅᔾᓂᖕᓕ ᐱᓯᔾᔾᑰ, ᐃᖃᓗᐃᑦ ᑕᖅᕿᕋᑯᕋᔾᖅ. ᓇᑲᓱᒃ ᐃᓕᓐᓂᐊᕐᕿᕋᖕᓕ ᓯᑕᒪᐅᔾᐊᖅ ᐃᓕᓐᓂᐊᕐᕿᐊᑕᖅᑲᑕᐅᕐᕿᖅ ᐃᓕᓐᓂᐊᐊᕐᕿᖅᑕᑐᐊᑦ ᐃᖃᓗᖔᓂ. ᐃᓕᓐᓂᐊᕐᕿᖕᑉ ᐊᑎᖅᑲᖅᑎᑕᐅᔾᖅ ᓇᑲᓱᒡᒥ, ᐱᒡᐊᖅᑎᑎᐃᐅᓯᑕᐅᖅᖔᑎᖕ ᐃᖃᓗᖔᓂ.

Iqaluit is the territorial capital of Nunavut, and is the largest and fastest-growing community in the territory, with a population of 7,250. It is known as the government, transportation, journalism, and business hub of the territory. Iqaluit is also rich with both traditional and contemporary Inuit culture. It has many rolling hills, as well as tundra valleys and rocky outcrops, and the tides of Frobisher Bay (also the former name of Iqaluit) are the second highest tides in Canada. The northern lights are frequently seen here from October to April. In the summer, days in Iqaluit are long and sunny, averaging sixteen hours of daylight, with almost twenty-four hours of sunshine in late June and only four hours of daylight in December. Because of the bay, Iqaluit often experiences heavy fog.

Nakasuk School is one of four elementary schools in Iqaluit. The school is named after Nakasuk, the founder of Iqaluit.

The Howl of the Wolf

Scotty Monteith, Age 10, Grade 5

It was a stormy night. It was the night before the wolf came out. If the storm lasted until the day after tomorrow we would be saved. But if it doesn't, someone will have to save the town from the wolf. If that person doesn't, all of us will have to sacrifice ourselves to the wolf to stay alive.

Then we heard a knock at the door. My brother went to the door to check who was there. But no one was there. He opened the door and someone was laying there. He had lots of frostbite on his face. He had a map to the wolf's den. He tried to walk but he couldn't. Then he said, "Kill the wolf for me."

Me and my brother set out for the wolf. The map was confusing. The map showed us to go through the iceberg and then Devil's Bridge. But how could we cross Devil's Bridge with all of the ghosts flying around it?

We brought a radio with us. "The weather forecast for today is -50 at Rankin Inlet." My brother said to me, "It's going to be very windy tonight." We were hoping that we would survive the wind. It was hard, he died. I arrived at Devil's Bridge. I was scared, I survived the bridge. It was almost time. I got there in time. The wolf was almost out of the cave. I got out my gun. The wolf dodged my shots. Finally I killed the wolf and I went home to tell my dad the news that I killed the wolf.

ᐊᒪᕈᑉ ᒥᐊᒡᒎᕐᓂᖓ

ᓯᑳᑎ ᒫᓐᑏᑦ, 10-ᓂᒃ ᐅᑭᐅᓕᒃ, ᒍᕇᑦ 5

ᐅᓐᓄᐊᒃᑯᑦ ᐱᖅᓯᖅᑐᐊᓗᖕᒥ. ᐊᒪᖅᑯᐃᑦ ᓯᓚ ᓄᐃᓚᐅᖅᑎᓐᓇᒋᑦ ᐅᓐᓄᐊᖓᓂ. ᐱᖅᓱᓐᓇᖅᐸᑦ ᓯᓚ ᖃᐅᒧᑦ ᐱᐅᓕᔭᐅᔪᓐᓇᖅᑐᒍᑦ. ᑕᐃᒪᐃᙵᒋᑉᐸᑦᑕ, ᐊᒪᖅᑯᓂᑦ ᓄᓇᒋᔭᕗᑦ ᑕᐅᓐᒋᔭᕗᖅ ᓴᐳᔾᔪᐅᒥᐊᓕᒃ ᐊᒪᖅᑯᓂᑦ. ᑕᐃᓐᓇ ᐃᓄᒃ ᑭᓇᑭᐊᖅ ᐱᙱᑉᐸᑦ, ᑕᒪᐃᓐᓇᐅᔪᑦ ᐊᒪᖅᑯᒧᑦ ᑐᓂᕆᐊᖅᑲᖅᑐᑦ ᐊᒪᕈᖅ ᐆᒪᕐᑯᑦᑐᒍ. ᑐᓴᖅᑐᑦ ᑎᒡᓗᒃᑐᖅᑐᒥᒃ ᒪᑐᒃᑯᑦ. ᐊᖓᔪᒐ ᐹᓚᐊᕐᒪᑦ ᑕᑯᔭᖅᑐᖅᓱᓂ ᑭᓇᐅᖕᒪᖔᑦ. ᐱᑕᖃᕋᓂ ᑕᐃᑲᓂ. ᐹ ᒪᑐᐃᕋᒥᐅᒃ ᑕᐃᑲᓂ ᓇᑦᓚᖓᔪᒥᒃ ᑕᑯᑦᑐᓂ. ᑮᓇᖓᒍᑦ ᑯᐊᖅᓯᒪᓂᖃᖅᑐᒥᒃ ᐊᒥᓯᓂᒃ. ᓄᓇᙳᐊᓕᔭᖅᑐᖅ ᐊᒪᖅᑯᑉ ᓯᑎᖓᓄᑦ. ᐱᓱᓕᓱᒃᑲᓗᐊᕋᒥ ᐊᔪᖅᓱᓂ. ᑕᐃᒪᓕ ᐅᖃᓯᕗᖅ, "ᐊᒪᕈᖅ ᑐᕐᑯᑕᐅᓚ ᐅᕙᖓ ᐱᔾᔪᑕᐅᓗᖓ."

ᐅᕙᖓ ᐊᖓᔪᒐᓗ ᐊᒪᕈᖅᓯᐊᕆᐊᓯᕗᒃ. ᓄᓇᙳᐊᖅ ᓇᓗᓇᕈᓘᔭᖅᑐᓂ. ᓄᓇᙳᐊᖅ ᒪᓕᒃᑕᕗᑦ ᑕᐃᑯᓇ ᐱᖃᓗᔭᓚᐊᖄᑦᓚᒡᓗᑕ ᐅᖓᑖᓄᑦ ᓵᑖᓇᓯᐅᑉ ᐃᑳᕈᑎᖓᓄᑦ. ᖃᓄᑦᓚ ᑖᓐᓇ ᐃᑳᕐᕕᒃ ᐊᑎᓕᒃ ᓵᑖᓇᓯᐅᑉ ᐃᑳᕈᑎᖓᓄᑦ ᐃᑳᕈᓐᓇᖅᐱᑎᒍᑦ ᐸᐃᔫᖅᑲᐅᕋᒪᑦ?

ᓈᓚᐅᑎᒥᒃ ᓇᒃᓴᖅᓱᑕ. "ᐅᑦᓗᒥ ᓯᓚᐅᑉ ᖃᓄᐃᓐᓂᖓ -50-ᐅᔪᖅ ᑲᖏᖅᖠᓂᕐᒥ." ᐊᖓᔪᒐ ᐅᕙᓐᓄᑦ ᐅᖃᖅᓱᓂ, "ᐅᓐᓄᒃ ᐊᓄᓂᔪᐊᓘᓚᖓᔪᖅ." ᐊᓐᓇᐅᒪᔭᓐᓇᓂᐊᒃᓴᖅ ᐊᓄᓂᒥ ᖃᓄᑎᒋ ᐱᔪᓐᓇᕐᒪᖕᒫᑦᑕ ᐃᓯᒪᓕᖅᑐᖓ. ᑐᕐᑯᑦᑕᓗᓂ. ᑎᑭᓐᓇᒪ ᓵᑖᓇᓯᐅᑉ ᐃᑳᕈᑎᖓᓄᑦ, ᑲᑉᐱᐊᓱᒃᖢᖓ, ᐊᓐᓇᒃᖢᒍ ᓵᑖᓇᓯᐅᑉ ᐃᑳᕈᑎ. ᐱᕙᓴᖓ ᑎᑭᑉᐳᖅ. ᐊᒪᕈᖅ ᑎᓯᒥᓂᒃ ᐊᓂᓕᖅᑐᖅ. ᖁᑭᐅᑎᓕ ᖁᑭᐅᑎᓕ ᑎᒍᑦᑐᒍ. ᖁᑭᓇᐊᖐᖓᒃᑯ ᐊᒪᕈᖅ ᐊᒡᕚᖅᑕᖅᓱᓂ. ᐊᓯᐃᑖᒃ ᐊᒪᕈᖅ ᑐᖁᑉᐸᖓ ᐊᖏᖅᖓᐅᑦᑐᖓᓗ ᐊᑖᑕᓕ ᐅᖃᐅᑎᑦᑐᒍ ᐊᒪᖅᑯᓚᐅᕐᓂᖓᖅᓱᖓ ᐊᒪᖅᑯᒥᒃ ᖁᑭᖅᓯᓚᐅᖓᒪ.

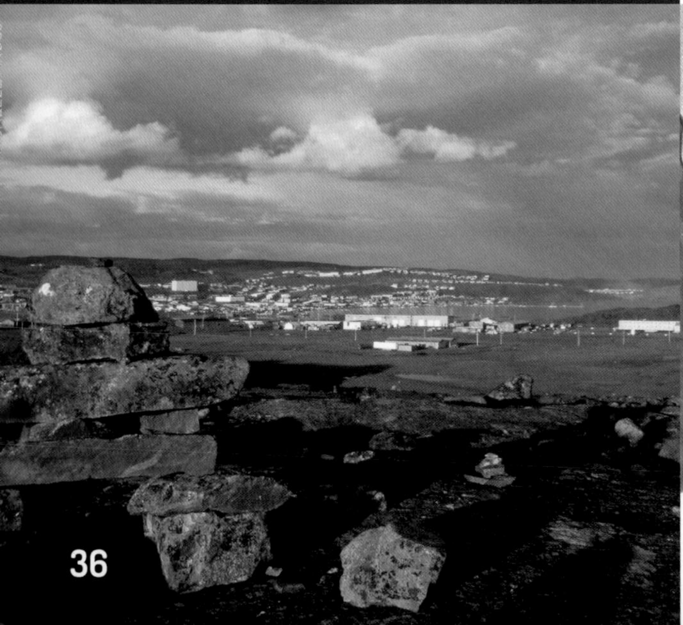

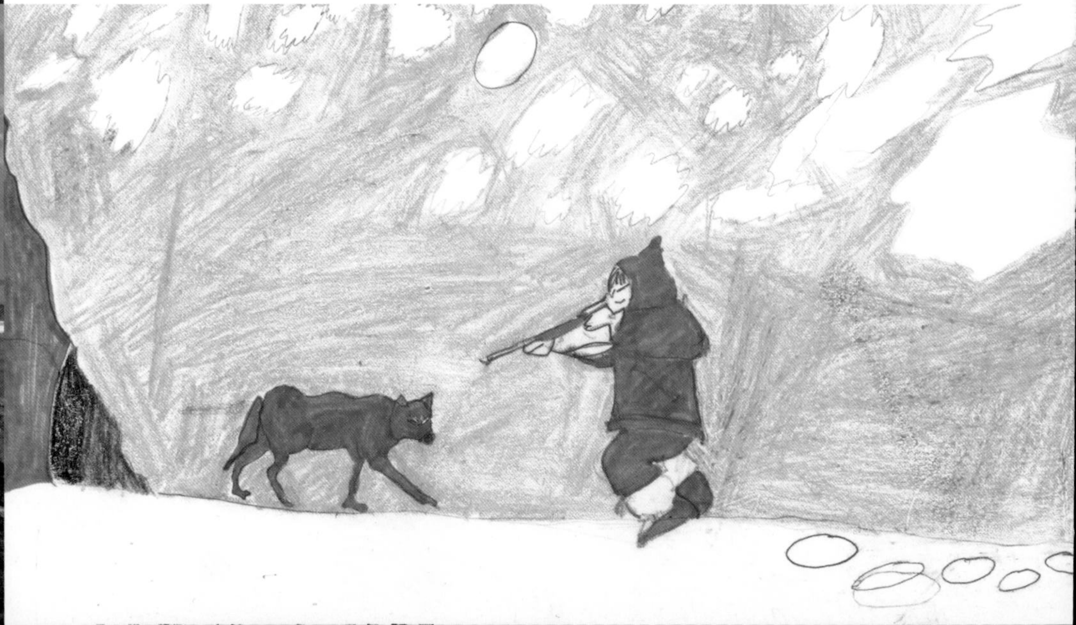

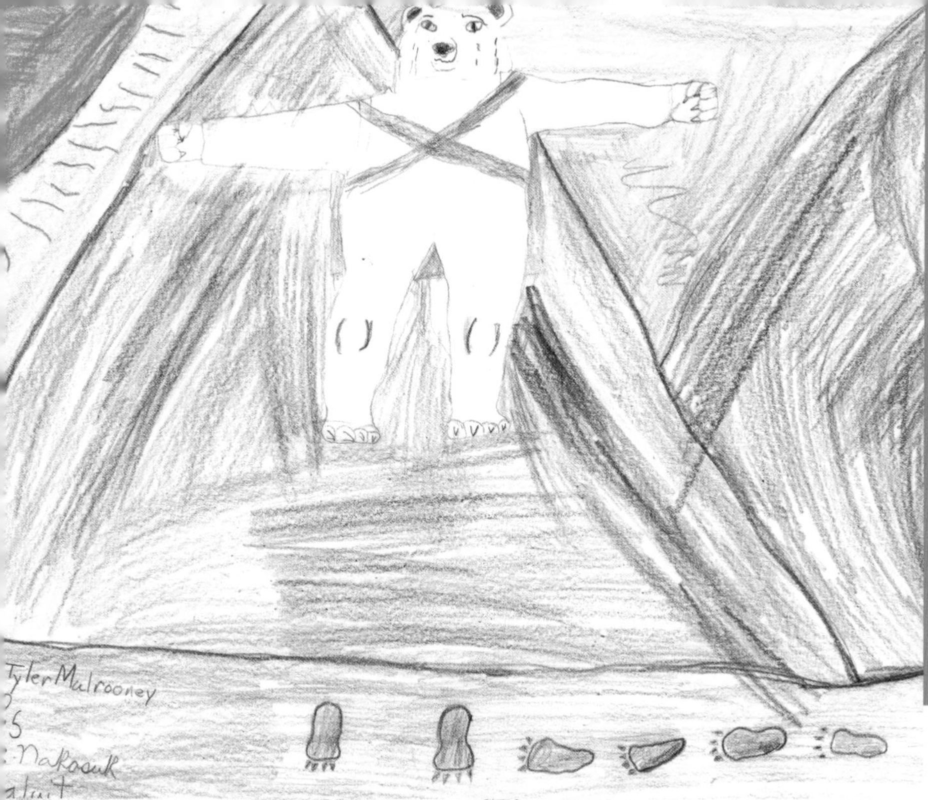

a Qamaniq, Age 10, Grade 4

ᐃᓴ ᖃᒪᓂᖅ, 10-ᓂᒃ ᐅᑭᐅᓕᒃ, ᒍᕌᑦ 4

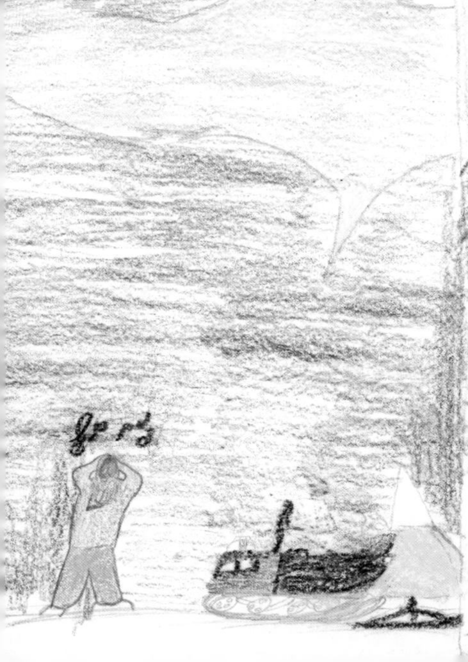

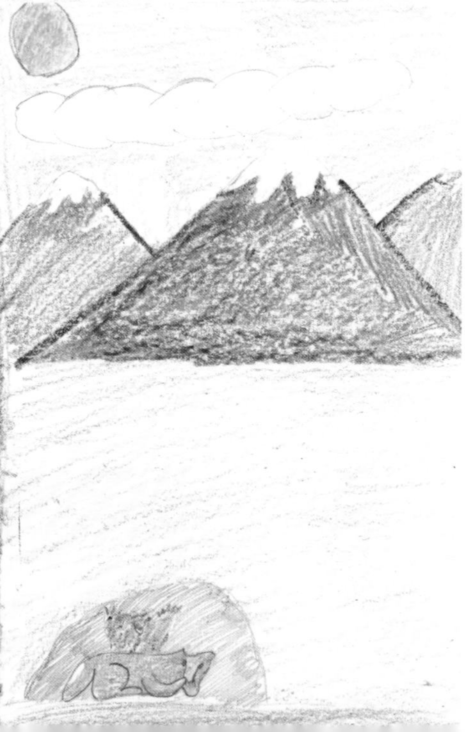

The Polar Bear Who Wanted the Sky

Tyler Mulrooney, Age 10

One day Tom the Polar Bear wanted the sky. He wanted the sky so bad he tried catapulting himself up to it but he failed. The polar bear tried flying up and grabbing it, but he went up too far and fell down.

The next day his friend asked him, "Why do you want to have the sky?"

"I want to have the sky to water my garden."

"What are you growing?" he asked.

"Tomatoes," Tom said.

"Why do you want tomatoes?"

"I need them for ketchup for hamburgers."

Then his friend said the sky is for everyone.

The next day it rained and Tom got his tomatoes.

ᓇᓄᖅ ᓯᓚᒥᒃ ᐱᔪᒪᓚᐅᖅᑐᖅ

ᑕᐃᓗ ᒪᑦᕉᓂ, 10-ᓂᒃ ᐅᑭᐅᓕᒃ

ᐅᑦᑐᑉ ᐃᓚᖕᒐᓐᓂ ᑖᒻᒥᒃ ᐊᑎᓕᒃ ᓇᓄᖅ ᓯᓚᒥᒃ ᐱᔪᒪᑦᑕᓕᖅᑯᖅ. ᓯᓚᒥᒃ ᐱᔪᒪᓗᐊᕐᓂᑯᒥᓄᑦ ᖁᒻᒧᑦ ᒥᓯᖅᑲᑦᑕᓯᕗᖅ ᑭᓯᐊᓂᓕ ᐊᒻᒧᑐᐃᓐᓇᖅᐸᒃᓱᓂ. ᖁᒻᒧᑦ ᑎᖕᒥᓇᓱᑦᑕᕋᓗᐊᕋᒥ ᓯᓚᒥᒡᓗ ᑎᒍᓯᓇᓱᒃᓱᓂ ᐊᒻᒧᑦ ᑲᑐᐃᓐᓇᖅᐸᒃᑕᖅᐳᖅ.

ᖃᐅᖓᒻᒪᑦ ᐃᓚᓐᓇᖓᑕ ᐃᓚᖓᑦ ᐊᐱᕆᓪᓗᓂ, "ᓲᖅᑕ ᓯᓚ ᐱᔪᒪᑦᑕᖅᐱᐅᒃ?"

"ᓯᓚ ᐱᔪᒪᔭᕋ ᐃᒻᒥᖅᑎᑉᐸᖕᓂᐊᕋᒃᑯ ᐱᕈᓯᐃᕝᕕᒐ."

"ᓱᓇᓂᒃᑕ ᐱᕈᖅᓱᐃᒐᕕᑦ? ᐊᐱᕆᓪᓗᓂ.

"ᑐᒫᑐᓂᒃ," ᑖᒻ ᑭᐅᓪᓗᓂ

"ᓲᖅᑕ ᑐᒫᑐᓂᒃ ᐱᔪᒪᕕᑦ?"

"Hᐋᒻᐳᒍᓄᑦ ᑳᒃᓴᑉᒥᒃ ᐱᖅᑲᓇᐊᖅᑲᖁᒪ."

ᐃᓚᓐᓇᖓᑕ ᑭᐅᓪᓗᓂᐅᒃ ᓯᓚᑕ ᑕᒪᐃᓐᓄᑦ ᐱᒋᔭᐅᔪᖅ.

ᐅᑦᑐᒃᑲᓐᓂᐊᓂ ᓯᓚᓗᖕᒪᑦ ᑖᒻ ᑐᒫᑐᑖᕐᓂᖅᐳᖅ.

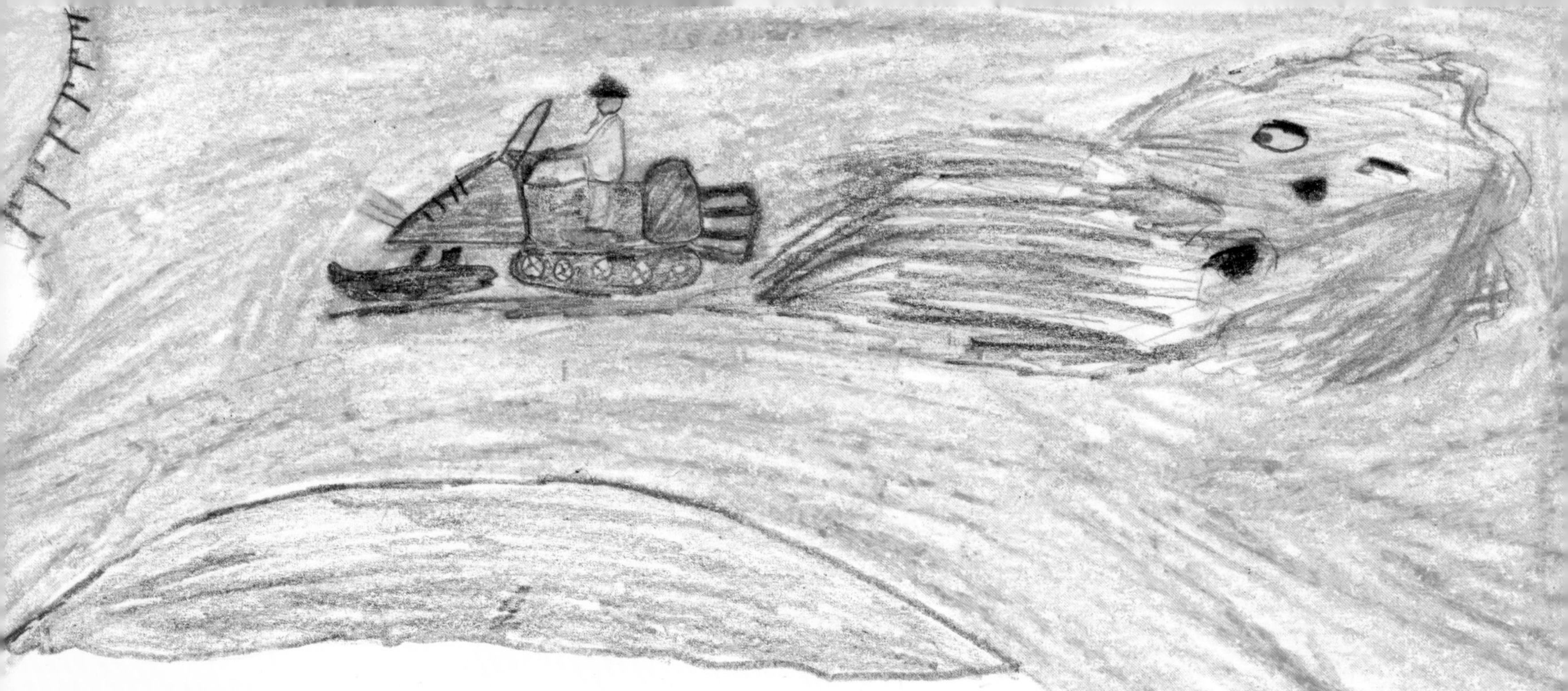

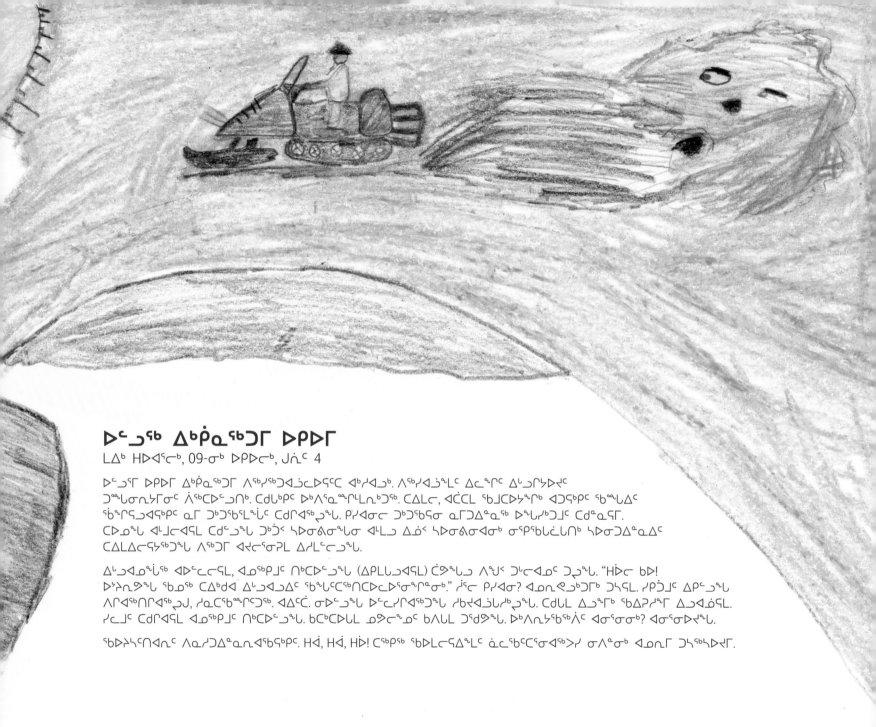

ᐅᑦᑐᖅ ᐃᒃᑰᓇᖅᑐᒥ ᐅᑭᐅᒥ

ᒪᐃᒃ ᕼᐅᐊᕐᓚᒃ, 09-ᓂᒃ ᐅᑭᐅᓚᒃ, ᒍᓅᑦ 4

ᐅᑦᑐᕐᒥ ᐅᑭᐅᒥ ᐃᒃᑰᓇᖅᑐᒥ ᐱᖅᓯᖅᑐᐊᔾᔭᓚᐅᕋᑦᑕ ᐊᒃᓯᐊᑐᒃ. ᐱᖅᓯᐊᔾᔪᖕᒪᑦ ᐃᓚᖏᑦ ᐃᒡᓗᒋᔭᐅᔪᑦ ᑐᙱᓂᕆᔭᒥᓂᑦ ᐋᖅᑕᐅᑦᑐᑎᒃ. ᑕᑯᒃᑭᑦ ᐅᒃᐱᕐᓇᙱᒻᒪᕆᒃᑐᖅ. ᑕᐃᒪᓕ, ᐊᑖᑕᒪ ᖃᒧᑕᐅᔭᖏᒃ ᐊᑐᕋᒃᑭᑦ ᖃᙵᐃᑦ ᖄᖏᕋᑐᐊᕋᒃᑭᑦ ᓇᒥ ᑐᒃᑐᖃᕐᒪᖔᑦ ᑕᑯᒋᐊᖅᑐᖓ. ᑭᓯᐊᓂᓕ ᑐᒃᑐᖃᕋᓂ ᓇᒥᑐᐃᓐᓇᖅ ᐅᖓᓯᒃᑐᒧᑦ ᑕᑯᓐᓇᕋᒥ. ᑕᐅᓄᖓ ᐊᒧᓕᐊᕋᒪ ᑕᑯᑦᑐᖓ ᑐᒃᑑᑉ ᓴᐅᓂᕚᓂᖓᓂ ᐊᒻᒪᑐ ᐃᓅᑉ ᓴᐅᓂᕚᓂᐊᓂᒃ ᓂᕈᕐᑲᒐᓛᒐᑎᒃ ᓴᐅᓂᑐᐃᓐᓇᐃᑦ ᑕᐃᒪᐃᓕᕋᔭᖅᑐᖓ ᐱᖅᑐᒥ ᐊᔪᓕᕐᓂᕈᒪ ᐃᓯᒪᓪᓚᑐᖓ.

ᐃᒡᓗᐊᓄᖕᒌᖅ ᐊᐅᓪᓚᓕᕋᒪ, ᐊᓄᖅᑭᒧᑦ ᑎᒃᑕᐅᓪᓗᖓ (ᐃᑭᒪᒐᓗᐊᕋᒪ) ᑖᕗᖓᓗ ᐱᖑᑉ ᑐᒡᓕᐊᓄᑦ ᑐᕌᖓ. "ᕼᐆᓕ ᑲᐅ! ᐅᔾᔨᕆᕗᖓ ᖃᓄᖅ ᑕᐃᒃᑯᐊ ᐃᒡᓗᐊᓗᐃᑦ ᖃᖓᑦᑕᖅᑎᑕᐅᓚᐅᕐᓂᖏᓐᓂᒃ." ᓃᕐᓕ ᑭᓯᐊᓂ? ᐊᓄᕆᕙᒃᑐᒥᒃ ᑐᓴᕋᒪ. ᓯᑰᔪᑦ ᐃᑭᑦᑐᖓ ᐱᒋᐊᖅᑎᒋᐊᖅᑕᐅᒍ, ᓱᓇᑕᖅᑲᙱᑦᑐᖅ. ᐊᐃᑦᑖ. ᓂᐅᑦᑐᖓ ᐅᑦᑕᓯᒋᐊᖅᑐᖓ ᓱᑲᔪᐊᔾᔪᒪᓱᒃᑕᖓ. ᑕᑯᒪᒪ ᐃᓗᕐᒥᒃ ᖃᐃᕆᓱᕐᒥ ᐃᓗᐊᓅᕋᒪ. ᓯᓚᒧᑦ ᑕᑯᒋᐊᕋᒪ ᐊᓄᖅᑭᒧᑦ ᑎᒃᑕᐅᓪᓗᖓ. ᑲᑦᑕᐅᒪᒪ ᓄᕗᓕᖕᓄᑦ ᑲᐱᒪᒪ ᑐᕐᑯᕗᖓ. ᐅᒃᐱᓇᔭᖅᑲᖅᐹᑦ ᐊᓂᕐᓂᓂᒃ? ᐊᓂᕐᓂᐅᔪᖓ.

ᖃᐅᔨᓴᕐᑎᐊᓇᑦ ᐱᓇᓱᑐᐃᓐᓇᓇᐊᖅᑲᖅᑭᑦ. ᕼᐋ, ᕼᐋ, ᕼᐆ! ᑕᒃᑯᒃ ᖃᐅᒪᓕᕋᐃᖕᒪᑦ ᓈᓚᖅᑲᑦᑕᕐᓂᐊᖅᐳᓯ ᓂᐱᓐᓂᒃ ᐊᓄᓂᒥ ᑐᓴᖅᓴᐅᔪᒥ.

Melodie Sammurtok, Age 9, Grade 4
ᒪᓬᑎ ᓴᒻᒧᕐᑑᖅ, 09-ᓂᑦ ᐅᑭᐅᓕᒃ, ᒍᕆᑦ 4

Jennifer Loubert, Age 10, Grade 5
ᔭᓂᕙ ᔫᕉᑦ, 10-ᓂᑦ ᐅᑭᐅᓕᒃ, ᒍᕆᑦ 5

One Cold Winter Day
Mike Horlick, Age 9, Grade 4

One cold winter day in my hometown we had a terrible blizzard. We had such a bad one that the next morning some of the houses were blown right off their supports. When I found this out I could hardly believe my eyes.

So, that morning I got on my dad's Ski-Doo and drove out past the mountains to where all the caribou are. But when I got there I couldn't see a caribou for miles around. I drove down the hill and saw a skeleton of a caribou and a man picked clean. My guess was that the wind had picked the bones clean. Then I thought what would happen if I got caught in it.

I turned around, and a huge gust of wind picked up my Ski-Doo (with me on it) and carried it all the way to the top of the next hill. "Holy cow! Man, now I think I know how those houses got lifted up." But why? I heard another gust of wind heading my way. I got on the Ski-Doo and turned it on, nothing. Dang. I got off and ran as fast as I could. I saw a cave and got in it. I looked outside and got caught in the gale. It dropped me into a pit of spikes and I died. Do you believe in ghosts? I'm one.

Watch out, I'm coming to haunt you. Ha, ha, ho! Listen every full moon for my wail in the Arctic wind.

ᑐᓗᒐᖅ

ᒥᓗᑎ ᓴᒻᒧᒃᑐᖅ, 09-ᓂᒃ ᐅᑭᐅᓕᒃ

ᑐᓗᒐᖅ ᑎᒡᓕᒍᒪᔪᖅ ᓯᕿᓂᕐᒥᒃ,
ᖃᓄᑭᐊᖅ ᓇᓚᐅᑦᑎᕆᐊᖃᕋᔭᖅᑐᖅ,
ᑕᐃᒪᐃᑉᐸᑦᓕ ᖃᓄᐃᓐᓂᐊᓕᖅᐱᑕ?
ᐃᓕᓐᓂᐊᕐᕕᖃᓐᖏᓕᕋᔭᕐᒪᑦ ᖃᐅᒪᓂᖃᓐᖏᑦᑐᓂᑐ,
ᑖᖅᑐᒥᒃ ᓯᓚᕐᔪᐊᖃᓕᕋᔭᖅᑐᒍᑦ ᓯᑐᐃᓐᓇᕐᒥᒃ ᐊᐳᑏᓐᓇᕐᒥᒡᓗ,
ᐊᑲᐅᒐᔭᖅᐳᒍᑦ ᐊᔪᓕᕐᓂᖅᐸᑦ ᐱᓇᓱᒃᑕᒥᓂᒃ
ᐃᒃᑮᖑᔪᒥᒃ ᐅᖅᑰᔪᒥᓗ ᓯᓚᕐᔪᐊᖃᕋᔭᖅᑐᒍᑦ.
ᑐᓗᒐᖅ ᐸᕐᓇᓕᓇᑦ ᐊᓂᖅᓵᖅᐸᒡᓗᑎᒃ ᐊᐅᒃᑲᕐᓂᕐᓗᑎᑦᓗ,
ᓈᓴᓚᐅᖅᑕ ᐱᖕᒐᓱᒧᑦ ᑎᑭᑦᓗᑕ,
1, 2, 3,
ᑕᐃᑲᐅᓕᖅᐳᖅ,
ᐊᓂᖅᓵᖅᑐᐊᓘᑦᓗᓂ ᐊᒻᒪᓗ ᐊᐅᒃᑲᖕᒐᑦᓗᓂ,
ᐊᒻᒪᓗ ᓴᐱᓕᖅᐳᖅ,
ᑕᐃᒪᓐᓇ ᐱᔾᔪᑎᒋᑦᑐᒍ ᓱᓕ ᓯᕿᓂᖃᖅᐳᒍᑦ,
ᐊᒻᒪ ᑐᓗᒐᖅ ᑲᙳᓱᓕᖅᑐᖅ ᓱᓕ.

Raven

Melodie Sammurtok, Age 9

Raven wants to steal the sun,
somehow he will have to guess,
but if he does what shall we do?
For there will be no more school and no more light,
we will live in a black dark world full of ice and snow,
we will be in luck if he does not make it,
we'll live in a cool and warm world.
Raven get ready to puff and sweat,
let's count to three,
1, 2, 3,
there he goes,
just puffing and sweating,
and he's given up,
that is why we still have the sun,
but the Raven still feels shamed.

Why the Arctic Fox is White

Ryan Henderson, Age 9, Grade 4

On a cold winter day in the cold Arctic, there were two foxes. Their names were Tim and Andrya. One day Tim said, "I will go out and fetch us some delicious food."

"O.K., my love. But be careful not to get lost."

Tim nodded his head, and went outside. While Tim was outside he noticed that it was quiet. He said to himself, "Maybe a blizzard is coming."

Tim thought for a moment. Then he said out loud, "Well then, I'd better hurry and get some food."

Tim was right about them having a blizzard. All the animals were in their dens. The wind was blowing the snow around.

Back at the den Andrya started to worry about Tim. Tim was also worried, because he thought he would never find any food. The weather was getting worse. Now you could not see where you were going. Each time Tim took a step the snow would stick to his feet. When Tim finally found a den, he got in and cooled off.

After he had warmed up, he tried to shake the snow off himself. But it stuck there! He tried again and again. But it still stuck there. Tim was quite tired from fighting through the wind, so he fell asleep. When he woke up he heard a voice calling his name so he looked outside. The blizzard had cleared up so he went outside to try to shake off the snow. And there sat Andrya weeping.

"Don't cry, my love," said Tim.

Andrya looked up. "Go away!" she said.

"It's me, Tim," said Tim.

"Is it really you?" asked Andrya.

"Yes it is," said Tim.

"But you're so, so, white!" said Andrya.

Then Tim remembered. After he explained everything to Andrya, Tim tried to get the snow off himself again. Not even a teaspoon of snow came off him. It was stuck on for good, and forever. And that is why the Arctic fox is white.

ᐱᖅ ᑎᓕᓂᐊ� ᖅᑯᖅᒪᖑ�](C

ᕳᐃᕚ ᒧᐃᒍᑦᖏ, 09-ᓂ�b ᐅᑭᐅᓕᒃ, ᒍᐱᑦ 4

ᐅᑭᐅᒧᓕᐊᑐᖕᒥ ᐃᖃᖃᖕᒍᒥ ᐅᑭᐅᖅᑕᖅᑐᒥ, ᒪᕐᔪᖕᓂ�b
ᑎᓕᓂᐊᖅᑕᐅᖅᑐᖕᖅ. ᐊᑎᖁ� ᑎᒥ ᐊᒡᓗ ᖃᑐᓇᐊ. ᐅᓪᓚᐪ ᐃᓇᓕᓂ ᑎᒥ
ᐅᖃᖕᓇᓂ, "ᐊᐃᖕᢉᓂᐊᑲᖕᢉᓪᓇ ᓂᖅᑭᑎᐊᖮᖕᖮb ᒪᒪᖕᢉᒥᖮb."

"ᐉᖕ, ᓇᒻᒐᓐᓚ. ᖃᢉᐊᖓᓐ ᐊᢉᐅᑦᑕᐅᑦᓐᖮᕳ."

ᑎᒥ ᐊᖕᢉᑎᖕᢉᓂ, ᐊᒷᓚᐪ ᢉᓚᢉᒐᖕᢉᓂ. ᑎᒥ ᐊᓂᢉᒡᓐᢉᓂ ᐅᢉᢉᓇᕗᖕᖮb
ᢉᓇᢉᐃᢉᓈᐉᐊᑦ ᓂᐱᖕᖮb ᒻᒣᖮᢉᖕᖮᑦᑦ. ᐃᒻᒔᓚᐪ ᐅᖕᢉᖕᖮᓂ, "ᐅᖕᢉᢉᓂᐊᓂᢉᓚᖕᖮᑲᐃᓚ."

ᑎᒥ ᐃᢉᓞᓐᓀᓐᢉᐅᖕᖮᓂ. ᓂᐱᒹᓄᐪᐪᓐᐉᐪ ᐅᖕᢉᖕᖮᓂ, "ᐊᢉ, ᑍᐊᖕᢉᢉᓐ
ᢉᓇᢉᖕᖮᢉᖕᢉᐅᑎᐊᖕᖮᑲᢉᖕ."

ᑎᒥ ᐊᢉᐃᐬᖮb ᢉᓐᢉᓂᢉᖕᖮᖕ ᐊᖕᢉᖕᖮᓂᐊᓂᢉᓐᖮᐪ. ᑏᐃᐬᐨᖮᐪ ᐅᐪᢉᐊᐪ
ᑎᓐᒹᖮᖮᢉ. ᐊᐪᓂᓂᐪ ᐊᖕᢉᖕᖮᢉᖕᢉᓂ ᓇᐨᒍᐃᖕᖮᐪ ᐊᐪᒍᓂᐪᐊᓂᓂ.

ᑍᐃᖮᓐ ᑎᓂᐨᖮᖮᖮᐪ ᢉᐪ ᢉᓇᑐᓐᐊ ᑎᓂᖕᖮb ᐃᢉᐪᑐᐨᖮᐪᖕᖮ>ᖮb
ᐊᖕᢉᑎᢉᖮᐪᓂᐪᖮb. ᑎᒥ ᐃᐪᒥᖮᑲᐪᐅᖕᖮb ᐃᢉᐪᑐᐨᢉᖕᖮᐪ
ᢉᓇᢉᖕᖮᢉᢉᐊᒪᖮᖕᖀ. ᢉᓇᐪ ᐃᐪᐅᐪᖮᑎᖕᖮᐪᐨᐨᐊᐪᐪᓂ. ᢉᐪᒪᐪᐪ
ᓇᐨᒍᐃᖮᖮb ᑏᐨᐪᐪᑎᐊᢉᖮᐪᖕᖮᐪᐨᐊᐪᐪᓂ. ᑎᒥ ᒪᐪᢉᐪᐨᒍᖕᒥ ᓇᐪᐪᐪᖮᐪᐪ
ᑐᑲᐃᢉᖕᖮᐪᐪ ᐊᐪᖕᖮᐪᐪᑐᖮb ᐃᢉᐪᖕᖮb. ᓇᢉᢉᑏᐪᖮᐪᐪᐪᖕᖓᒥ ᑎᐪᒪᖮb, ᐃᐪᐪᐊᐪ
ᢉᐪᐪᖮᓂ ᐅᖮbᢉᢉᒐᖮᖕᖮ>ᖮᖮᐪᓂ.

ᐅᖮbᢉᐪᐊᐪᖮᐪᐨᓂ, ᐊᐪᑏᐃᐪᖕᖮᐪᖕᖮ>ᖮᖮᐪ. ᖃᢉᐊᖓᓐ ᐃᢉᐪᢉᐃᐨᐪᐪᖮb ᐊᐪᐪᑫ!
ᐃᖮᕳᖮbᐨᐨᐪᐪᐨᐊᐪᒥᖮb ᐃᢉᐪᢉᐃᐨᐪᐪᖮb ᐊᐪᐪ. ᑎᓐᐨ ᑏᖮbᢉᓐᒣᐪ ᓞᖮbᐃᢉᒥ
ᐊᓇᐨᖮᑖᐨᐅᐪᖀ, ᢉᓇᐪᖕᖮᓂ. ᑐᖮbᐪᒥ ᐊᑏᒥᖮb ᑍᐃᐪᐊᐪᓞᒣᐪ ᢉᢉᐪᐪ
ᑍᑮᐨᖮᖕᖮᖕ. ᐃᖮbᑐᒤᖮᐪᐪᖕᖮᖀ ᢉᢉᐪᐪᖕᖮᐪᐪ ᐊᐪᑏᐃᐪᑎᐊᖮᐪᖮᐪᖮb.
ᑍᐃᐨᐪ ᢉᓇᑐᓐᐊ ᐃᐪᢉᖮᐪᐪᓂ ᖃᢉᐊᖮᐪ.

"ᖃᢉᐊᖮᐨᐪᑎᖮb, ᓇᒻᒣᖮᐪᐪᑐᖮb," ᑎᒥ ᐅᖮbᖮᐪᐪᓂ

ᢉᓇᑐᓐᐊ ᢉᒡᓐᒍ ᖃᢉᐊᖮᐪ ᐅᖮbᖮᖮ>ᖮb, "ᐊᢉᖮᐪᐪᑏᐪᑫ!

"ᐅᖮᐪᓐ, ᑎᒥ," ᑎᒥ ᐅᖮbᖮᐪᐪᓂ.

"ᐃᖮᐅᐪ ᐅᐪ?" ᐊᐪᓐᐪᐪᐪᓂ ᢉᓇᑐᓐᐊ.

"ᐃᐪᐨ ᓞᖮbᐃᢉᒥ," ᑎᒥ ᖁᐅᐨᐪᐪᓂ

"ᑏᐪᐨᐪᐪ ᖮbᐪᖮbᐪᒣᓐᓞᐊᐪᓞᐃᐪᕳ! ᢉᓇᑐᓐᐊ ᐅᖮbᖮᐪᐪᓂ.

ᑎᓐᐪ ᑍᒪ ᐃᖮbᐃᐪᐪᖮb. ᐅᖮbᐅᐪᑏᐪᐅᖮbᐪᐪᐪᐪᖮb ᢉᓇᑐᓐᐊ,
ᐊᐪᑏᐃᐪᖮᐪᐪᐪᖮᐪᖮb ᢉᐪᖮbᖮᐪᖮb. ᖃᢉᐊᖮᐪ ᐊᐪᒥᖮb ᐊᐪᖮᒍᐪ
ᑏᑏᐨᑎᐪᖮbᖮᐪᐪᒥᖮb ᐃᖮbᐪᖮbᖮᐪᐨᒣ. ᐃᢉᐪᢉᐃᐨᐪᐨᐪᐪᓂ, ᑍᐃᐪᖮᖖᐪᑏᐪᐨ.
ᑍᐃᐪᖮᐪᐪ ᐪᢉᐨᐪᐪᖮᐪᒍ ᑎᓕᓂᐊᐪ ᖮbᐪᖮbᐪᖖᐪᐪ.

Iqaluit: Nakasuk School   41

ᐊᕐᕕᐊᑦ	Arviat
ᑎᑭᕋᕐᔪᐊᖅ	Whale Cove
ᑲᖕᒋᖅᖠᓂᖅ	Rankin Inlet
ᑭᙵᐃᑦ	Cape Dorset
ᐃᖅᑲᓗᐃᑦ	Iqaluit
ᐸᖕᓂᖅᑑ	Pangnirtung
ᓇᓂᓯᕕᒃ	Nanisivik
ᒥᑦᑎᒪᑕᓕᒃ	Pond Inlet
ᐃᒃᐱᐊᕐᔪᒃ	Arctic Bay
ᖅᑲᐅᓯᐅᑦᑐᖅ	Resolute Bay
ᐊᐅᔪᐃᑦᑐᖅ	Grise Fiord

ᐸᖕᓂᖅᑑᖅ
ᐊᑕᒍᔪᒃ
ᐃᓕᓐᓂᐊᕐᕕᒃ

Pangnirtung
Attagoyuk Ilisavik
High School

ᑖᓐᓇ ᓄᓇᓕᒃ ᐃᓄᖅᖅᑑᖅ 1,550-ᓂᒃ ᖃᐅᔭᕐᒐᐅᑎᑕᐃᒃᖃᖅᑑᖖᐊᒄ ᓴᓇᖖᒍᐊᕐᕓᖖᓯᓂ ᓴᓇᖅᐅᖅᖅᑑᑎᒃ Lᒄᖖᑭᖅᙳᖃᐃᐃᖅᕐᖅᖅᔪᒪᖅᕓᔮᑯ ᐊᒄᖓ ᑎᑎᖅᖅᑐᒃᒻᔩᖅᒄ. ᐅᔅᑳᑐᓕᔫᑊᒄ ᐅᓐᔮᖅᖅᑑᑭᒃ Lᔮᕐᖅᑎᓐᒃ ᐊᒄᖓ ᔳᖅᒅᓂᖅᖅᑎᑭᔮᖅᖅ. ᐅᑑᖅᒃᑑᖅᒃᐳᒻᒣ, ᐊᑎᖔᓕ ᐸᖕᓂᖅᑑᔮᕐ, ᑑᑭᒄᕐ "ᑖᐃᓂ ᐸᖕᓂᖅᑊ" ᑖᐃᒪᖖᐊ ᐅᖅᖄᑕᐅᑕᐅᓯᓂᖅᑎᒄ ᐊᔾᓈᖖᑎᑎᒄ ᐊᑎᑭᖔᒻᒃ ᐊᑕᒍᔳᖔᒃ ᐊᕓᖅᒍᔮᒃ 100 ᐅᔮᓕᑖᒃᓯᐅᑕᖅᖅᖅᖅᖖ ᑑᔮᐃᒄ ᔮᓂ ᐊᖅᖅᑎᖅᒃᒃᐅᑎᑭᖅᖅᑎᒄᓇᓕᔮᒄ ᐅᒄᓂᒻᐃᔮᖅᖅ ᐊᒻᓯᖖᒄᑎᒃᖖᓂᒄ ᐃᓄᒃᒃᒄᐊᑭᐅᑎᑕᖅᖅᑎᑕᖖᒄ ᔮᓐ. ᐸᖕᓂᖅᑑᔮᕐ ᓇᒻᖅᖖᐃᓕ ᐃᒪᐅᐃᐃᑕᖅᖅ 50 ᐊᒻᒥᖓ ᐱᖅᖖᓇᖖᓂᒄ ᐅᖔᐅᖅᖅᖔᑊᐳ ᐃᓂᖖᔳᐊᖖᓂᖅᒃ, ᖃᖅᖅᖅᒣᒃ ᖄᖔᓂᒃ. ᐃᔾᐃᖖᐃᐅᑊᖖᒄ ᐊᐅᔮᐃᖅᑊᖔᐳᖅ ᒣᖖᔳᐃᒄᔳᖅᔳᖖᓴᒻᒄᒄ. ᑖᖅᖅᖅᒥᒄ ᐊᑕᐅᔳᒻᒄᒃᒣ, ᐸᖕᓂᖅᑑᖅᖅ ᔳᔮᖔᓂᔳᖅᑑᖅᖅ ᐅᖔᐅᔳᖔᒃᒄᖅᖅᖅ ᐃᐃᖅᖅᓂᒄ 24-ᓂᒃ. ᑖᓇ Hᐊᓕᒄ ᐱᖅᖅᒻᒄᐊᔮᖅᖅᑑᖅᖅᖅ, ᐊᒄᖓ ᐅᖅᐅᒣ ᐃᑊᖅᐊᖖᓂᖅᖅᐳᖖᐊᖅᖅᑑᖅᖅ ᑎᖅᒻᒄᒄ ᐃᑊᐱᖖᐊᖖᓂᖅᒻ -60°C .

This community of 1,550 is known for its woven tapestries and lithographic prints, and is popular with hikers, climbers, and skiers. According to legend, the name Pangnirtung, which means "the place of the bull caribou," was given to the community by a hunter named Attagoyuk over one hundred years ago, before caribou had to change their migration patterns due to human encroachment. Located 50 kilometres south of the Arctic Circle, on a fiord in mountainous terrain, it is the southern gateway community to Auyuittuq National Park. For a month in the summer, Pangnirtung has twenty-four-hour sunshine. This hamlet can get extremely windy, and in the winter months with the wind chill factor, it can feel like -60°C.

Big Storm
Eeta Akulukjul

In early 70s, it was nice outside, the children were playing tag, and their mothers were sewing clothes for their husbands when the sun came down. When the children got cold, they went into the iglu and told their parents, "It is getting colder and snowy a little bit." The mothers' husbands were out hunting, the storm came here very fast. The mothers were shouting, "My husband, my honey," and the blizzard was there maybe for an hour. The storm calmed, the mothers were trying to make caribou stew after they finished sewing clothes for their husbands. It was still windy, one of the little boys was going to go outside for peeing. And he saw the people who were coming from out hunting. They walked slowly and feeling sad, and the little boy started running, and the little boy was so excited seeing his father coming. But when he saw him, he got sad because he was almost frozen and hurried to the iglu. After he got better he started going to hunt again, he learned his lesson from the storm.

The End.

ᐱᕐᑐᖅᑦᐅᕐᑦᐊᕐᓂᖅ
ᐄᑕ ᐊᑯᓗᒃᔪᓪ

ᑕᐃᓲᕐᒪᓂ 70-ᓂᖅ ᐊᕐᕋᔮᖕᖓᓂ, ᓱᓴᑎᐊᕐᐅᐸᖕᒪᓪᓕᑦ, ᓱᕐᓱᑦ ᐊᒻᒪᓗᐸᕐᖃᐸᕐᑕᐅᑎᓪᓗᓐᑭ ᐱᖕᖑᐊᕐᑐᖅᓯ, ᐊᒻᒪᓗ ᐊᖁᓇᖕᓂᒐ ᒦᖅᓯᐅᑎᓪᓭᒐᕐᑭ ᐅᐃᖕᒐᕐᑎ ᐊᓚᖁᑦᓴᕐᓂ ᓴᖅᓱᕐᓂᖅ ᐊᒡᔪᑦᔪᖅ. ᓱᕐᓱᑦ ᖁᑉᐅᑲᓇᒡᓚᑦ, ᐃᓪᓗᐊᓂᓚᐊᖅᑲᑕᐅᑦᓗᓐᑭ ᐊᖁᓖᔫᔪᑦᐃᕐᓗᑦᐅᒐᐊᕐᓂᖅᖅ. ᐊᖁᓇᖕᒐ ᐅᐃᖕᒐᕐᑎ ᐅᐊᑯᐃᓚᑦᓚᑦ, ᓱᒃᑲᕐᐊᓪᒐᕐᒐ ᐱᖅᓱᕐᓯᐊᖅᐳᖅᓄᖅ. ᐊᖁᓇᐅᕐᑦᓚᑦ ᖃᐃᓚᕐᕋᕐᓂᖅᐳᕐᑦ, "ᐅᐊᓗ, ᓇᖕᓲᖅ," ᐊᒻᒪᓗ ᐱᖅᓱᕐᑐᐊᔨᔭᐅᒍᒍᓂ ᐃᓚᖕᓯᒐᖕᒃ ᐊᑕᐅᑦᓰᕐᒐᐅ. ᐱᖅᓱᓯᓇᒌᖕᖓᓚᑦ, ᐊᖁᓇᐅᕐᑎᒐ ᐅᑦᐅᓪᐅᑦᐃᖅᐳᕐᑦ ᑐᖕᒐᒐᕐᒃ ᒦᖅᓯᐊᓯᓇᒡᒐᕐᒃᐳᐊᕐᖕᒐ ᖅᓱᐊᕐᓂᒐ ᐊᖁᓇᖕᓂᒐ. ᓱᕐᑦ ᐊᕈᑦᓂᒍᓯ, ᖃᑉᓚᐊᕐᖕᓂ ᓱᕐᒐᓗᓐ ᖅᑕᐄᑦᓯᕐᑐᓯᖅ. ᑕᑦᓗᓂ ᐊᖕᔪᓇᕐᑲᖕᓂᒐ ᐅᖕᑕᐅᓪᐊᑦᓯᕐᑐᕐᓂᒐ. ᓯᓇᕐᐊᕐᓂ ᑕᑕᓗᓂᐊᕐᒐᑭᐊᕐᖅ ᖅᑕᐅᐊᕐᔪᒻᖅᓚᒐᑦᓄᑭᓂᒐ, ᖅᐳᕐᐊᔭᓐᖅᓂᒐ ᐊᑦᐅᕐᐅᓪ ᐃᓪᓗᐊᓂᓖᔪᑦ ᐃᓯᓇᐊᕐᓚᕐᑦ. ᐃᐱᓲᕐ ᐊᖕᓄᓇᕐᑉᖕᓇᑕᑎᐅᓂᒐ, ᐃᓚᑦᑐᐅᓂᒐᕐᓂᒐ ᐱᖅᓱᕐᑐᐊᓂᒐᕐᒍ ᖅᓇᖅ ᐱᔪᖕᓇᐊᕐᓯᕐᖅ.

ᑕᒪ ᐃᕐᐊ.

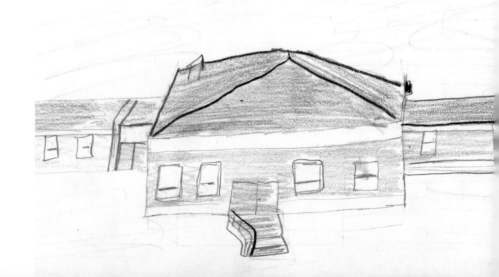

ᐊᑎᖅᖃᑎᑕᐅᖖᒌᕐᑕᑐᖅᖅ
[ᑎᑎᕋᐅᔅᖅ]

ᓇ ᐊᒃᐸᓕᐊᓗᒃ

ᕐᑯᑐᐃᕐᒪᐊᐃᑦ ᓄᓇᒋᓐᐊᖅᕐᑕᕐLᑕ
ᕿᕐᑭᓯᓂᖅᓴᐃᐊᖅᒪᕐᒐᑎ. ᐱᒪᔪᐊᕋᔾᔮᕐᑐᓗᒃ
ᐱᕐᒍᑉᒍᓐᒍᓗ ᐊᒍᑐᐃᔪᐊᕐᖅ. ᑕᐃᒪᖅᕿ
ᑭᒃᕕᕐᓇᖅᖃᖅ. ᐃᓄᐃᑦ ᐊᐅᓪᓚᑕᖅᕐᓯᕌᕐᔭᕐᒪᕐᒪᕐᒪᕐᑕ.

Untitled [Drawing]

Tina Akpalialuk

People go for a camping in the sunny day.
They play and they walk around. This is a
wonderful day. People like to go camping.

People go for a camping in the sunny day. they play and they walk around. this is wonderful day and. people like to go camping.

Untitled [Drawing]

This is in middle of July. We went blueberry picking. My dad was coming and when he was coming he saw a seal and he was trying to catch it. It was a nice sunny day. My mom and Sheila are picking berries. I was at the boat with my sister and nephew. We had fun. It was a nice and very hot day.

ᐊᑎᖅᖅᑎᑕᐅᖕᒥᑕᑐᖅ

ᑖᓐᓇ ᑜᑕᐄᒃ ᖅᐱᑎᖕᖠᓂᐅᑲᑕᐅᖅᑯᖅ. ᑭᔪᑕᖕᒃᓇᓂᒃ ᖃᑎᖅᕐᕈᑖᓗᑕ. ᐊᑖᑕᒪ ᑎᑭᑦᕝᒐᒥ ᓇᕐᖕᒐᒃ ᓇᐅᐱᑦᑎᐅᒥ ᐱᓇᓱᐅᕐᑕᑦᖅᐊᖕᓗ. ᕐᖅᐸᓂᑎᐊᖅᓗᓂ ᕐᓚ ᐱᐅᓗᓗ. ᑜᖅᖕ ᕐᓚᓗ ᑭᔪᑕᖕᒃᓇᓂᒃ ᓄᓃᖁᑎᓗᕐᖕ. ᐅᒥᐊᕐᕝᖅᑲᑕᐅᑦᓗᖕᒃ ᖁᑲᕐᓗ ᐊᕐᓗ ᓄᐊᕐ ᐃᓚᑕᐅᓗᖕ. ᖅᑯᐱᐊᓇᓯᑕᐅᖅᑯᖅ. ᕐᓚᑎᐊᖅᐸᑕᐅᖕᓂ ᐊᕐᓗ ᐅᖅᑯᔮᑎᑎᐊᖅᓗᖕ.

ᐸᖕᓂᖅᑑᖅᖅ: ᐊᑕᔪᖕᖅ ᐃᓚᖕᓂᐊᕐᑭ

is is in middle of July. we went BlueBerry
ny. my dad was coming and when he
s coming he saw a seal and he was
ing to catch it. It was nice sunny day.
y mom and Sheila are picking berries.
was at the boat with my sister and
hers. we had fun. It was a nice
y and very hot day.

47

⊲ˢ໖⊲ᑦ	Arviat
∩ᑭᕴˢᣞ⊲ᖅ	Whale Cove
ᑫᙯᒡᙯᐸᕐᓂᖅ	Rankin Inlet
ᑭᓈᔾᓴᐃᑦ	Cape Dorset
ᐃᖅᑲᓗᐃᑦ	Iqaluit
ᐸᖕᓂᕐᑑ	Pangnirtung
ᓇᓂᓯᕕᒃ	Nanisivik
ᒥᑦᑎᒪᑕᓕᒃ	Pond Inlet
ᐃᒃᐱᐊᕐᔪᒃ	Arctic Bay
ᖃᐅᓱᐃᑦᑐᖅ	Resolute Bay
ᐊᐅᓱᐃᑦᑐᖅ	Grise Fiord

ᓇᓂᓯᕕᒃ
ᐊᓪᓗᑐᑦ ᐃᓕᓐᓂᐊᕐᕕᒃ

Nanisivik
Allurut School

ᓇᓂᓯᕕᒃ ᐅᑉᓇᖃᒃᓂᐊᕐᐃᐅᑎᐅᖅᑐᖅ ᐊᖅᐳᖅᓯᖅ-ᕆᐊᖃᒥᒃ ᐊᒻᓗ ᐅᑉᓇᖃᒃᓂᐊᕐᕕᒃ ᓴᓇᔭᐅᑎᐅᖅᑐᖅ 1975-ᒥ ᒪᑐᔭᐅᓪᓗᓂᓗ 2002-ᒥ. ᖂᑭᔭᐅᑎᒡᓗᒍ, ᐃᓄᖅᑐᐊᖂᖃᑎᐅᖅᑐᖅ ᑕᒪᓂ 77-ᓂᒃ. ᑲᓇᑕᐅᑉ ᒐᕙᒪᖏᑦ ᐸᕐᓇᐃᓯᒪᓯᖅ ᐅᑉᓇᖃᒃᓂᐊᕐᕕᓕᓐᓂᐅᕐᒥᒃ ᐅᕝᐊᔪᔭᐅᖓᑦ ᐅᑉᓴᔭᑦᕆᖅᐅᑉᑰᑌᒡᒍ, ᓂᔾᓗ ᒪᑯᓈᓇ ᐅᕈᐅᖃᒃᑕᖅᒥ ᑎᑭᑦᑕᖅᑐᖓᑦ, ᐱᖁᓇᖃᒃᑕᐅᐊᖅᔪᕐᒥᔭᐅᖓᑦᐅᓂᓂ 2016-ᒥ.

Nanisivik was a lead-zinc mining and mineral processing community that was built in 1975 and that closed in 2002. At its height, this tiny community only had a population of 287. The Canadian government has plans to convert the abandoned community into a station for refuelling government ships, such as Arctic patrol vessels, with construction anticipated to finish in 2016.

© ARCTIC KINGDOM

ᑲᓪᓗᒃ

ᔫᓇ ᐊᕐᓇᕐᔪᐊᖅ, 07-ᓂᒃ, ᐅᑭᐅᓕᒃ

ᑲᓪᓗᒃ ᑲᓪᓗᒃ, ᖃᓄᐃᑉᐱᑦ? ᓈᒻᒪᒃᑐᖓ.
ᑲᓪᓗᒃ ᑲᓪᓗᒃ, ᖃᓄᐃᑉᐱᑦ? ᐱᙵᐊᖅᑐᖓ.
ᑲᓪᓗᒃ ᑲᓪᓗᒃ, ᖃᓄᐃᑉᐱᑦ? ᐱᙵᐊᕆᔭᕋ ᐊᖑᑎᙵᐊᖅ.
ᑲᓪᓗᒃ ᑲᓪᓗᒃ, ᖃᓄᐃᑉᐱᑦ? ᖁᙱᐊᖅᑐᖓ ᖁᙱᐊᕐᒥᒃ.
ᑲᓪᓗᒃ ᓱᑲᔪᐊᓗᖕᒥᒃ ᓴᖅᑭᕐᕙᐳᖅ, ᐃᓄᐃᑦ ᑲᐸᐊᓕᖅᐳᑦ.

ᖃᓪᓗᐱᓪᓗᖅ

ᑲᓛᒃ ᒎᑎᐄ, 07-ᓂᒃ ᐅᑭᐅᓕᒃ

ᖃᓪᓗᐱᓪᓗᐃᑦ ᐃᒪᕐᒦᑦᑐᑦ.
ᓱᕈᓯᑦ ᓯᓈᒥ ᐱᙵᐊᖅᐸᑕ ᖃᓪᓗᐱᓪᓗᕐᓄᑦ ᐱᔭᐅᓚᖓᔪᑦ.
ᖃᓪᓗᐱᓪᓗᐃᑦ ᓱᕈᓯᕐᓂᒃ ᑎᒍᓯᑦᑕᖅᐳᑦ.
ᓱᕈᓯᑦ ᐱᙵᐅᓇᐊᖃᙱᑦᑐᑦ ᓯᑯᒥ.
ᖃᓪᓗᐱᓪᓗᕐᒧᑦ ᐱᔭᐅᑐᐃᓐᓇᓇᐊᖅᑲᖅᑐᑦ ᐃᒪᕐᒨᔾᔭᐅᓗᑎᒡᓗ.

Lightning

Jonah Arnarjaug, Age 7

Lightning lightning, how are you? I am fine.
Lightning lightning, how are you? I am playing.
Lightning lightning, how are you? I am playing with my toy man.
Lightning lightning, how are you? I am watching a movie.
Lightning suddenly coming, people all get a fright.

Qallupilluk

Clark Gouthier, Age 7

The qalupilluit are in the water.
If the kids play on the edge of the ice the qalupilluit get them.
Qalupilluit grab children.
Children should not play on the ice.
The qalupilluit would take the child under the water.

© B&C ALEXANDER / ARCTICPHOTO

Untitled

Teresa Kanatsiak, Age 8

I like the falling snow.
I like to go sliding.
I like the sun because it is warmer.
I like winter because we play hide and seek in total darkness. I like to go fishing.
I like to go camping because getting there we go over bumps on the ice.
I like the rain because our hair gets wet.
I like the snow because we play snowballs.
I like early spring because we go ice hopping and we fall in the water.
I like spring because we get to go to Arctic Bay by Ski-Doo and go for tea on the land.

ᐊᑎᕐᑲᖅᑎᑕᐅᙱᑦᑐᖅ

ᑎᕇᓴ ᑲᓇᑦᓯᐊᖅ, 08-ᓂᒃ ᐅᑭᐅᓖᒃ

ᐊᓕᐊᓇᐃᒥᔭᕋ ᖃᓂᖅᑎᑦᑐᒍ.
ᐊᓕᐊᓇᐃᒥᔭᕋ ᓯᑐᕋᕐᓂᖅ.
ᐊᓕᐊᓇᐃᒥᔭᕋ ᓯᕿᓂᖅ ᐅᖅᑰᓯᓇᕐᓂᖅᓴᐅᓂᖓ.
ᐊᓕᐊᓇᐃᒥᔭᕋ ᐅᑭᐅᒃᑯᑦ ᐃᔾᖃᑦᑕᕈᓐᓇᕋᑦᑕ ᑖᑦᑎᐊᖅᑐᒥ.
ᐊᓕᐊᓇᐃᒥᔭᕋ ᐃᕐᖃᓗᒃᓯᐅᕈᓐᓇᕐᓂᖅ.
ᐊᓕᐊᓇᐃᒥᔭᕋ ᒪᕐᑲᐃᓕᕌᖓᑦᑕ ᓯᑯᒥ ᒪᓂᙱᑦᑐᒃᑰᕈᓐᓇᕋᑦᑕ.
ᐊᓕᐊᓇᐃᒥᔭᕋ ᓯᓚᓗᒃ ᓄᔭᑦᑎᓐᓂᒃ ᖃᐅᓯᓕᖅᑎᑦᑕᕋᒪᑦ.
ᐊᓕᐊᓇᐃᒥᔭᕋ ᐊᐳᑦ ᒧᖅᐸᓕᐅᕈᓐᓇᕋᑦᑎᒍ ᐊᐳᑎᒥᒃ.
ᐊᓕᐊᓇᐃᒥᔭᕋ ᐅᐱᕐᙵᓕᖏᕐᓂᖅ ᒪᐅᔭᕋᖅᔫᖓ ᐃᒫᖅᑕᖅᔫᑕᓗ.
ᐊᓕᐊᓇᐃᒥᔭᕋ ᐅᐱᕐᙳᖅ ᐃᒃᐱᐊᕐᔪᓕᐊᕈᓐᓇᕋᑦᑕ ᖃᒧᑕᐅᔭᒃᑯᑦ ᐊᒻᒪᓗ ᑏᑐᕐᓗᑕ ᓄᓇᒥ.

ᐊᕐᕕᐊᑦ	Arviat
ᑎᑭᕋᕐᔪᐊᖅ	Whale Cove
ᑲᖕᒋᖅᖠᓂᖅ	Rankin Inlet
ᑮᖕᒥᕈᑦ	Cape Dorset
ᐃᖃᓗᐃᑦ	Iqaluit
ᐸᖕᓂᖅᑑ	Pangnirtung
ᓇᓂᓯᕕᒃ	Nanisivik
ᒥᑦᑎᒪᑕᓕᒃ	Pond Inlet
ᐃᒃᐱᐊᕐᔪᒃ	Arctic Bay
ᖃᐅᓱᐃᑦᑐᖅ	Resolute Bay
ᐊᐅᔪᐃᑦᑐᖅ	Grise Fiord

ᒥᑦᑎᒪᑕᓕᒃ ᑕᑭᔪᐊᓗᒃ ᐃᓕᓐᓂᐊᕐᕕᒃ

“ᒥᑦᑎᒪᑕᓕᖕᒥᒃ” ᐃᓄᒃᑎᑐᑦ ᐊᑎᖅᑲᖅᑎᑕᐅᓪᓗᓂ, ᐃᓄᑦᖃᕐᕕᓂᖑᑦ ᑕᐃᑲᓂ ᐃᓗᕕᖅᓯᒪᔪᒥᒃ ᐃᓱᒪᕆᔭᐅᓪᓗᓂ ᐱᑕᖃᖅᓯᕆᔭᐅᓪᓗᓂ, ᒥᑦᑎᒪᑕᓕᐅᑉ ᕼᐋᒻᒪᓚᖓᑦ ᐃᓄᖃᖅᑎᕆᔪᖅ 1,300-ᓂᒃ. ᖃᑭᖅᑖᓘᑉ ᑲᓇᖕᓇᖕᖓᓂ ᓄᕗᐊᓃᑦᑐᖅ, ᖃᓂᒋᔭᖃᐅᖅᖢᓂ ᑲᖏᖅᖢᓄᑦ ᐃᓅᑭᓕᖕᓄᑦ ᐊᐅᔨᐃᑦᑐᓄᑦᓗ, ᑕᑯᔭᖅᑐᕆᐅᑦᑕᖅᖢᓂᓗ ᑑᓚᓕᖕᓂᒃ ᖃᓚᓗᒃᑲᓂᒃ. ᐊᖏᖅᑲᓇᔭᐅᔪᖅ ᑳᒃᑯᓄᖓ ᑐᓄᓂᖅ ᐊᖅᓴᖅᓃᑦ ᐱᙳᐊᖅᑎᓄᑦ. ᒥᑦᑎᒪᑕᓕᒃ ᐊᐅᔭᑦᑎᐊᖑᖃᖅᓯᖅᑐᖅ ᑭᓯᐊᓂᓕ ᐊᓄᓈᑐᔪᖅ, ᒪᖁᒐᔾᔭᖅᖢᓂᓗ, ᐊᒻᒪᓗ ᐃᓖᓐᓂᒃᑯᑦ ᐅᑭᐊᒥ ᐊᐱᖅᔪᐊᖃᑦᑕᖅᖢᓂ. ᓄᓇᓕᐅᔪᖅ ᐊᕿᓗᓕᒃ ᑭᙵᓂ, ᐊᓄᓈᑐᓗᐊᙱᓐᓂᖓᖅᑕᐅᓪᓗᓂ. ᓄᕕᐱᓈᐅᑉ ᖃᑎᖕᖓᓂᑦ ᔮᓐᓄᐊᓕᐅᑉ ᖃᑎᖕᖓᓄᑦ, ᒥᑦᑎᒪᑕᓕᒃ ᓯᖃᓂᖅᑲᑦᑕᙱᑦᑐᖅ.

Pond Inlet Takijualuk School

Known as Mittimatalik in Inuktitut, after an ancient person thought to be buried there, the hamlet of Pond Inlet has a population of 1,300. It is located on the northern tip of Baffin Island, near fiords, glaciers, and icebergs, and it is renowned as a vantage point for large pods of narwhal. It is home to the well-known Tununiq Arsarniit Theatre Group. Pond Inlet has mild summers but very windy, rainy, and often snowy fall weather. The community is sheltered by mountains, which reduce the wind chill. From mid-November to mid-January, Pond Inlet experiences no sunlight.

ᐊᑏᖅᖃᑎᕈᐊᖏᕐᑕᑐᖅ

ᓴᐃᓚᔅ ᐅᑏᒃ, 12-ᓂᒃ ᐅᑭᐅᓕᒃ

ᑕᐃᓯᓛᓄᑐᖃᐅᓂᖅᖑᖅ ᐃᑑᒐᒪ ᐅᖅᑲᐅᔭᑐᑕᐅᑎᒐᒻᒪ ᓯᓚᐅᑉ ᐊᓄᕌᐅᓪᓗ ᒥᑭᖁᓐᓄᑦ. ᐱᓴᒃᓯᐊᕐᒐᒪ ᓚᖅᑲᐃᕐᐊᖅᖁᓐᒪ ᑕᐃᓚᖏᑕᒻᖅ ᓄᖅᖂᒍᒻᖅ ᖅᓄᖅᖃᑦᑌᖅᒐᒻᒪ. ᓄᖅᖅ ᑖᖅᒥᓐᒪᒥᕐᑯ ᑐᐱᖅᖁᑦ ᐅᑎᖅᖃᑦᑕᖅᖁᒻᒪ ᐊᓄᓂᐊᕐᓯᒪᑦ ᖅᑲᐅᔭᐳᒃᒃ. ᐅᑐᓄᐊᖅᖅᑦ ᓯᓐᖅᓐᑏᖅᖁᒻᒪ ᐊᓄᓂᖅᖅᖅᐳᖅᖁᒻᒪ. ᑐᖅᖃᒻᖃ ᓯᖅᖂᖅᓂᖅᒍ ᐊᒻᒪᓗ ᐅᖅᑯᖅᔂᒥᖅᖅ ᓯᑦ. ᐱᓇᓱᐊᕉᑦ ᐊᖏᖅᖄᑦ᠀ᒎᓐ ᓄᖅᖅᔄᑦ ᑖᖅᓯᕐᑦᓕᑦ. ᐊᖏᖅᖄᑦᖅᒐᒪ ᐱᕙᓕᖅᓄᒐᒻ ᓇᕐᖅᖁᒻᒪ. ᐊᖏᖅᖃᖅᒐᒪ ᐊᖁᖅᐃᓐ ᐅᐱᔪᕐᑕᐅᑐᖅᒪ ᐱᕙᓕᖅᓄᒐᒻ ᓇᕐᖁᒻᒪ.

ᓯᓚ ᐱᒪᔪ ᓴᓪᖅᓴᕐᐊᓂᖅ

ᐄᒥ ᑭᓪᓕᑭᑏ, 14-ᓂᒃ ᐅᑭᐅᓕᒃ

ᑕᐃᓯᓚᓂᒍᑐᖅᑲᐱᒃᖅ ᐃᑉᓘᖅᑲᑐᖅᖁᑦᒍ ᐊᖅᒪᕐᖁᕙᓕᑎᐊ. ᐃᑉᓗ ᓴᓇᐅᔭᕈᕐᒍᖅᒃ ᖅᐸᒐᖅ ᖅᑲᑐᖃᒍ. ᖅᑲᖑᑐᐊᖑᒃᖅᑦ ᐱᖅᐱᖄᖁᓐ ᑕᐃᑖᖓᑦᑕᐅᖅᖅᑐᒍ ᐅᑐᓐᐊᓇᖅᖅᒍᖁᒍᑦ ᐊᐳᐱᖅ ᓯᓗᐊᕐᓂᖁᓐ ᐊᐸᓗᐊᕐᓂᖁᓐᓗ ᐃᑉᓗᐊᓗᐱᓐᖁᓐ ᐱᒃᖁᒍ.

ᐅᒪᓄᐊᖅᔪᒃᖏᑐᒍ ᐱᖅᓯᕐᓂᖁᒻᒪ, ᑐᒃᓗᖅᓴᖅᑦ ᐊᑎᐅᑎᒃᐅᑦ. ᑐᖅᐊᖅᖁᓐ ᐃᑉᓗᑐᐊᖅᐳᖁᓐ. ᑕᐃᑲᓄᒍ ᓯᓐᖁᓐ. ᐅᖅᔠᒃᖁᑦ ᑐᖅᒪᒪ ᓯᖅᖂᖅᓂ᠀ᑎᖅᖁᓐ ᐅᖅᔪᒻᒍᒻᒍ. ᑭᓯᐊᓂ ᐊᖅᑉᐅᖅᒥᓐᑐᖅᖅᓂᓯᑦ. ᐃᑉᓗᐊᓗᖅ ᒥᖅᖁᓂᓪᖅ. ᐊᑖᑲᓗ ᐃᑉᓗᐊᓗᑕᐅᖅᖃᒃᓂᓗᓗ. ᑖᖅᓕᒃ ᐃᑉᓗᐊᓕᐊᒪᖅᓂᖅ ᓇᒃᑦᑎᖅᒐᒥ, ᖅᐸᒃᖅ ᐃᑉᓗᑐᐳᑕᐃᒪᖅᓂᖁᒍ, ᐊᖅᓯᑦ!

ᐊᑏᖅᖃᑎᕈᐊᖏᕐᑕᑐᖅ

ᓯᓚ ᑲᖅᖁᖅ, 11-ᓂᒃ ᐅᑭᐅᓕᒃ

ᑕᐃᑲᓂ ᓄᓇᕐᑕᖅᖃᑦᑕᓐᓂ ᓯᓚᒥᒥ ᖅᑲᐅᔭᖅᖁᐊᖅᑲᖁᑕᐅᖅᖃᕐᒥᓕᑦ, ᑭᕐᐊᓂᒃ ᐃᓚᓇᒐᖅᑕᑦ ᐃᓚᖅᖅᓯᑎᐱ ᓯᓚᒥ. ᑭᓪᖅᓂᓂ ᓄᖅᖁᓪᑎᖅᐱᓯ ᐃᑦᖅᑲᐅᖅᖃᖅᐊᖅᓴᖅᑕᐅᖅᑦ ᐊᑕᓄ ᐅᑦᖁᖁᑦ 10-ᓄᒃ 15-ᓄᒃ. ᓄᖅᖁᖁᓐ ᑖᖅᖅᑐᖁᓐ ᑕᑐᔫᑕᑦ ᖅᑲᐊᖅᖅᑲᕐᐊᖅᔪᖁᓐ ᐊᖁᓐᓗ ᐳᖅᑐᖅᖃᖅᐊᕐᓄᑏᓐ, ᐅᒪᓄᐊᔪᑦ ᓯᓚᒍᒥᓄᐊᖅᖂᓐ ᖅᑲᐅᔭᓄᖁᖅᒃᖃᓯᖅ. ᑕᐊᐃᓕᐊᓐᒪᕐᖅᖅᐱᖅᐱ, ᖅᑲᐅᔭᓂ ᓯᓚᒍᑎᖅᐳᒥᖅᖅ. ᓯᓚᒍᑐᐊᖅᖅᑎᖅᒍ ᒥᖅᐊᖅᖅᐱᖅᓄ ᐊᖅᒪᓗ ᐊᖅᒥᖅᖅᐱᖅᓄᖅ ᓄᖅᖁᖅᖃᒃᖂᓐᖅᖁᒍ ᐱᓯᐊᖄᖅᐳᒍᒍ, ᑭᕐᐊᔪᑦᖁᓗ ᒥᖅᐳᒃᖅᓂᖁᓐᖅ, ᑕᐊᒪ ᑲᕐᓂᖅᓄᐊᖅᔪᑕᑦᒍ. ᐊᖅᒪᓄᖅᖁᓕᑦ ᐅᓄᖅᖅᖄᐅᐳᖅᖅᖃᖅᑐᑦ ᐃᒪᖁᓇ. ᑕᐊᒪᑎᒍᖅ ᒪᖅᑲᐃᖁᓯᒥ ᖅᒍᖁᐳᖅᖁᑦ ᐃᑦᖁᓐ ᐱᖅᑎᒃᓄᐊᖁᑐᐃᕐ. ᐊᖅᐳᑕᐅᕐᕐ ᑐᖅᖂᖅᑦ. ᐅᖅᖃᖅᖁᓐ ᐃᒪᓇᒎᖅ ᑲᐳ ᐊᑐᐳᑕᐅᖁᑦ ᑐᖅᖁᖅᖃᖅᑐᑦ ᖅᑲᓄᒐ ᑕᑐᐊᖅᒎᕐᒥ ᓄᖅᖁᖅᓕᕐᕐᓄ ᑲᓇᖅᖅᒥ ᐊᖅᒪᓗ ᐱᖅᖁᖅᖁᒥ ᐊᓄᓐ ᐊᖁᓐᒎ ᑭᑎᖅᑲᑦ.

ᑕᒪᖅᖁᓇ ᖅᑲᐅᔭᖅᖁᓐᖁᐊᖅ.

Untitled

Silas Otik, Age 12

A long time ago my grandfather talked to me about weather and wind. Every time when I went hunting or camping I would always look for clouds. When the clouds got darker I went to my tent fast because I knew it would get windy. When I was sleeping at night the wind came. When I woke up the sun was shining and the weather was warm. Later on I was going back home because the clouds were getting darker. When I was going home I shot three seals. When I got home my mother was happy that I shot three seals.

Weather Contest

Amy Killikitee, Age 14

Long ago there was an iglu near our camp. The iglu was made out of wood by a kabloonak. Whenever there was a storm we used to go there to be safe because the igluvigak we had was so soft.

So one night the storm started, we all woke up. Immediately I ran to the iglu. I slept there. When I woke up in the morning and I went out it was sunny and hot. But there was a big problem. The igluvigak was broken. So my father had to make one again. When my dad got tired of making the igluvigak, he made an iglu out of wood, at last!

Untitled

Sheila Katsak, Age 11

Where we live there is no weather station, but elders study the sky. Mountains with a scuffy little cloud mean it's going to be cold under that cloud for ten to fifteen days. If we see grey clouds that look like they are coming and going higher, it's going to rain at night. If not, tomorrow it is going to rain. If there are small and big rain drops then it stops then starts, stops and starts, then there's just small raindrops, then there might be lightning. An elder told us a story. He said he was going camping by dogsled with his grandpa. They heard thunder. He said it was like clouds that looks like they are ripping like a cloth when they look up. If we see clouds and oval sideways on North and South then the wind is coming from the east.

That's all I know.

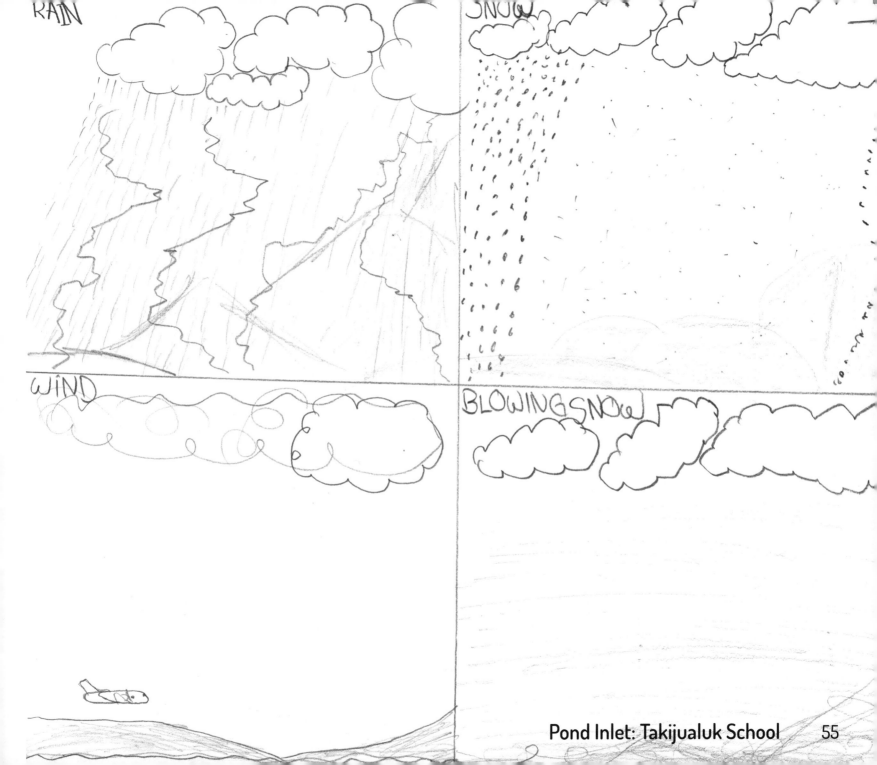

RAIN

SNOW

WIND

BLOWING SNOW

ᒥᑦᑎᒪᑕᓕᒃ: ᑕᑯᕝᕚᔪᖅ ᐃᓇᖕᓂᐊᕐᖕᖠᖅ

ᓯᓚᒃᓴᕆᔭᐅᓂᕐᒥ ᐊᔾᖑᒥᓂᖃᕐᐸᖅ

ᑖᓐᓇ ᑲᑦᓴᒃ, 15-ᓂᒃ ᐅᐱᐅᑎᒃ

ᐊᔾᖑᒃᔪᐊᑕᐅᖅᒃᑕᒐ ᑐᑭᖃᖅᑐᖅ
ᐊᓈᓇᒃᓴᖏᑦ ᓯᓚ ᓯᓚᒃᔭᐊᒥᒃ
ᐊᖏᑐᖅᓇᐅᑕᓐᓐᖀᒻᒃᐸ. ᐅᒪᔪᐊᑦ ᐃᓗᐊᓂ
ᖅᑲᐅᔨᓚᕿᖅᓈᖅᑐᑦ ᓇᑐᖅᐅᑐᑦ. ᐃᓯᖄᒍ
ᖅᐸᔾᖅ ᔮᓐᐸᐅ ᖅᐸᒃᖁᓂᖕᒃᓂᒍ ᐱᓐᓗᒍ
ᔭᐅᓐᓐᓐᐊᓂᖅᓗ.

ᐊᑕᓂ, ᓇᕝᖅᑐᖅᒃᖄᑦ ᐃᐅᐊᓐᓐᒃᔭᖿᑦ
ᐊᑕᓂ, ᓇᕝᖅᑐᖅᖿᖃᖅᐊᑦ ᐃᐅᐊᓐᓐᒃᔭᖿᑦ,
ᑭᓪᓐᓐᓇᒃᖄᓂ ᐅᐱᐅᖅᑕᖅᑐᒍᑦ
ᓂᕝᕝᐱᓐᓐᐊᕝᑕᖅᖅ, ᑕᓐᐅᓐᓗ ᐳᖅᑐᓂᖕᒃᓂ
ᐳᖅᑐᕝᒃᐸᓐᓐᐊᑦᓗᓐᒍ.

Contest Winner
Dawn Katsak, Age 15

My poster is depicting mother nature with the earth just out of her reach. The animals within her are confused. The eye is crying, reflecting God's sadness and disappointment.

Below the forest is burning, the ice is melting, the tree line is moving north and the water is rising.

ᐊᕐᕕᐊᑦ	Arviat
ᑎᑭᕋᕐᕈᐊᖅ	Whale Cove
ᑲᖏᖅᖠᓃᖅ	Rankin Inlet
ᑭᖕᖓᐃᑦ	Cape Dorset
ᐃᖃᓗᐃᑦ	Iqaluit
ᐸᖕᓂᖅᑑ	Pangnirtung
ᒥᑦᑎᒪᑦᑕᓕᒃ	Pond Inlet
ᒥᑦᑎᒪᑦᑕᓕᒃ	Nanisivik
ᐃᒃᐱᐊᕐᔪᒃ	**Arctic Bay**
ᖃᐅᓱᐃᑦᑐᖅ	Resolute Bay
ᐊᐅᔪᐃᑦᑐᖅ	Grise Fiord

ᐃᒃᐱᐊᕐᔪᒃ
ᐃᓄᔭᖅ ᐃᓕᓐᓂᐊᕐᕕᒃ

Arctic Bay
Inuujaq School

ᐃᒃᐱᐊᕐᔪᒃ ᕼᐋᒻᒪᓚᐅᔪᖅ 750-ᓂᒃ ᐃᓄᒃᑕᖃᐅᖅᖢᓂ, ᑲᓇᖕᓇᖕᒐᓂ ᐅᐊᖕᓇᖅᐸᓯᖕᒐᓂ ᕿᑭᖅᑕᕐᔪᐊᑉ. ᐃᒃᐱᐊᕐᔪᐊᑉ ᓄᓇᖕᒐ ᑕᑯᒥᓇᖅᑐᒥᒃ ᓄᓇᓕᒃ—ᓇᖅᓴᓕᒃ, ᐊᐅᐸᖅᑐᓂᓪᓗ ᐃᓐᓈᕈᖃᐅᖅᖢᓂ, ᐊᒻᒪᓗ ᑕᑯᒥᓇᖅᑐᓂᒃ ᑲᖕᒋᖅᖢᓂ ᐃᓐᓈᕈᓕᖕᓂᒃ, ᑖᓐᓇ ᐱᖃᑕᐅᑦᑐᓂ ᓵᓐᓂᕈᑎᐅᑉ ᑐᓄᓂᕈᓯᐅᑦᓗ ᐃᒪᖕᒐ, ᑕᑭᓂᖅᐸᐅᑦᑐᓂ ᑲᖕᒋᖅᖢᒃ ᓯᓚᕐᔪᐊᓕᒫᒥ. ᒪᐃᒥᑦ ᐱᒋᐊᖅᖢᓂ ᐋᒎᓯᒧᑦ ᑕᕿᖕᒐᓄᑦ ᑎᑭᖦᖢᒍ, ᐃᒃᐱᐊᕐᔪᒃ ᖃᐅᒪᕚᒃᑐᖅ ᓯᕿᓂᖅ ᓂᐱᒍᓐᓀᖅᑎᑦᓗᒍ. ᓄᓇᖕᒐᑕ ᖃᓄᐃᓐᓂᖕᒐ ᒪᓕᒃᖢᒍ, ᐊᕙᓗᔭᐅᓯᒪᓂᖕᒐ ᑭᖖᒐᕐᓄᑦ ᐅᖅᑰᐊᓕᓂᖃᕐᓂᖕᒐᓗ ᐊᓄᓇᕐᔪᐊᓂᑦ, ᓄᓇᓕᐅᑉ ᓯᓚᖕᒐ ᐊᓯᔾᔨᖅᑕᓗᐊᖕᒋᑦᑐᖅ.

ᐃᓄᔭᖅ ᐃᓕᓐᓂᐊᕐᕕᒃ ᐃᓕᓐᓂᐊᓕᓵᓂᑦ 12-ᓄᒃ ᐳᖅᑐᓂᕐᒧᑦ ᑎᑭᑦᓗᒍ ᐃᓕᓐᓂᐊᖅᑐᓕᒃ 240-ᓂ ᐊᒥᓰᔪᑦ ᖃᓂᒋᔭᖕᒐᓂᑦ.

Arctic Bay is a hamlet of 750 people, located at the northwest corner of Baffin Island. The hamlet is marked by dramatic terrain—deep valleys, sheer red rock cliffs, and beautiful fiords, including nearby Admiralty Inlet, the longest fiord in the world. From May to August, Arctic Bay experiences twenty-four-hour sunshine. Due to its unique topography, being surrounded by three substantial hills that protect it from harsh north winds, the community has a pleasantly stable climate.

Inuujaq School is a K–12 school with about 240 students.

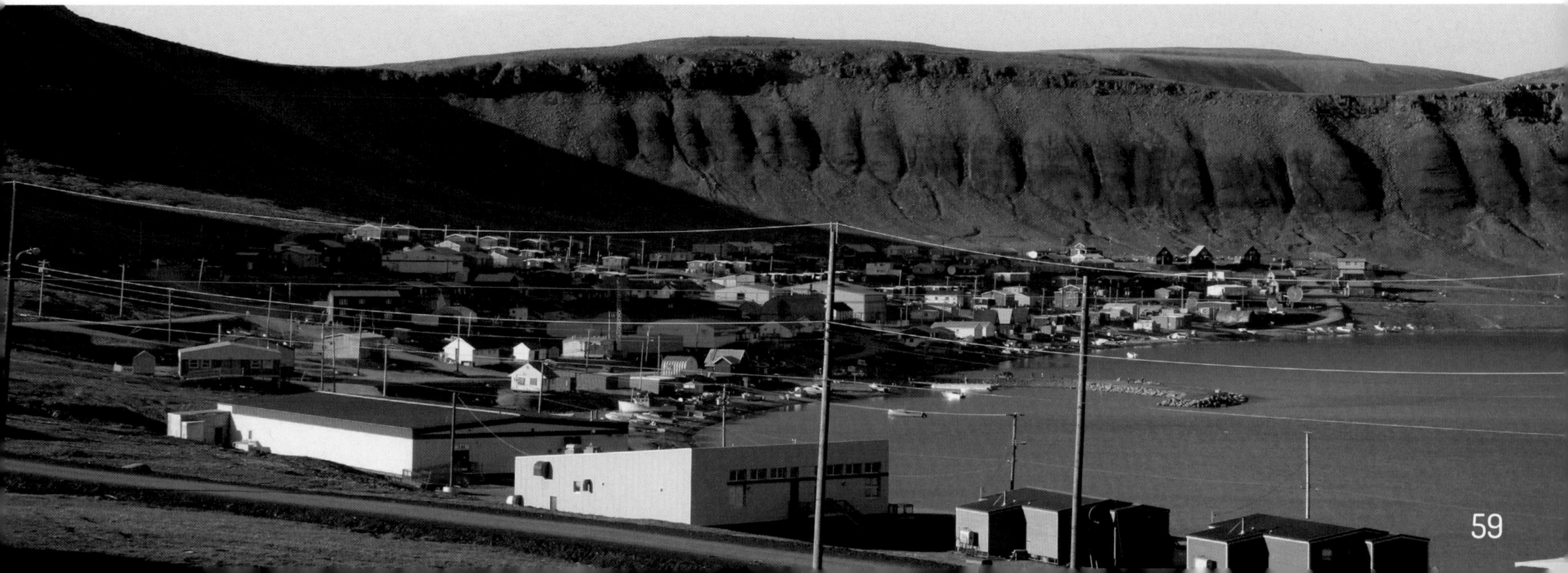

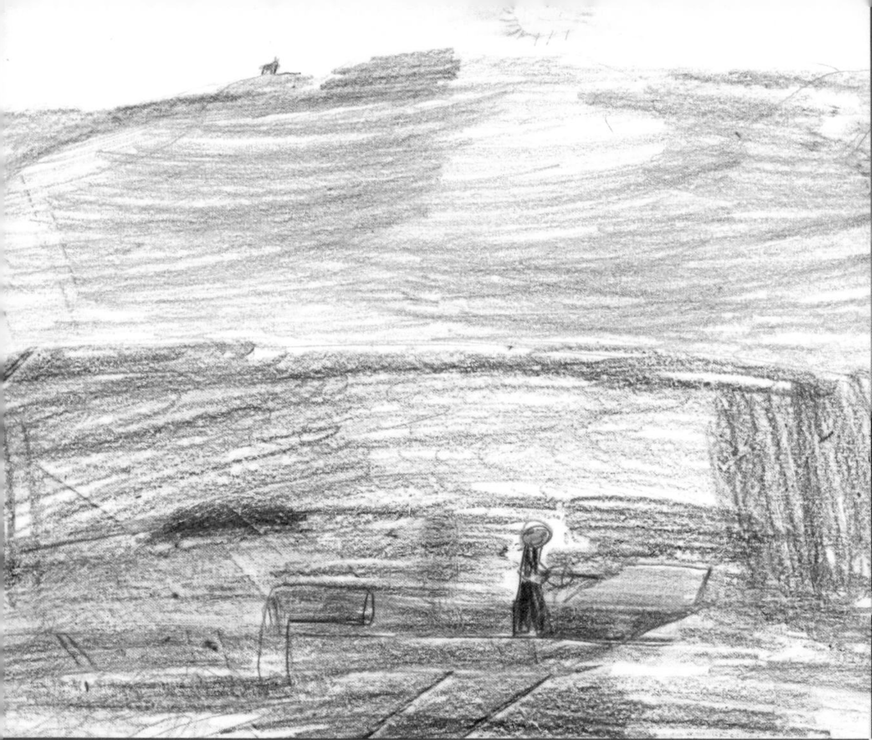

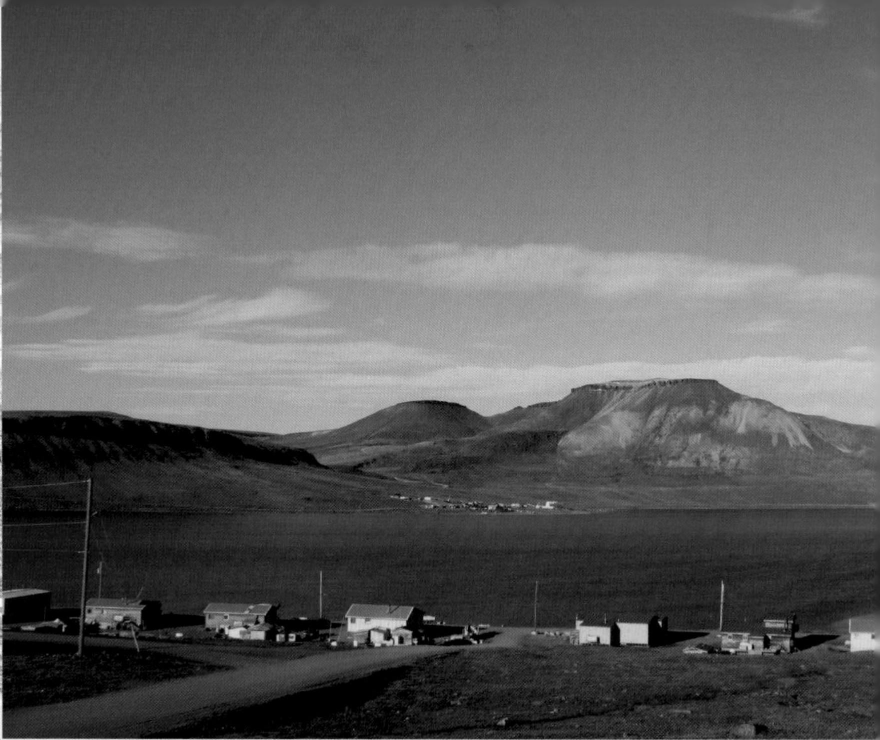

ᐊᑎᖃᖅᑎᑕᐅᙱᑦᑐᖅ

ᕗᐃᓐ ᑕᖅᑐ, ᐊᕐᕌᒍᓕᒃ 9, ᒍᓇᑦ 4

ᐊᓄᕌᔭᖅᓗᓂ ᐃᒃᑮᕌᓘᔪᖅ, ᕿᐅᓐᓈᓗᖕᒪᑦ ᐊᒻᒪᓗ ᒪᓪᓕᕐᔪᐊᖅᓗᓂ. ᔮᓐ ᓄᑐᒃᑯᑦ ᓄᓇᓕᖅᑖᖑᓚᐅᖅᓗᑕ ᐊᓄᓇᐊᓗᒻᒧᑦ ᔪᐃᓕᐅᑉ ᓇᓴᖓ ᑎᒃᑕᐅᓪᓗᓂ. ᐅᑎᓕᖅᓗᑕ ᓄᓇᖕᒐᓄᑦ ᒪᓪᓕᓗᐊᖅᑐᐊᓘᓕᕐᒪᑦ ᑕᐃᑯᙵᕋᑦᑕ ᑐᐱᖅᓗᑕᓗ ᐃᑯᓪᓚᖅᑰᓪᓗᑕ ᖃᐅᒃᐸᙳᕐᒪᑦ ᑕᒪᐅᙵᐅᓕᓇᓪᓗᑕ ᐃᒃᐱᐊᕐᔪᖕᒧᑦ ᒪᓪᓕᒃᑐᖏᓐᓂᖅᓴᐅᓪᓗᑕ.

Untitled

Wayne Taqtu, Age 9, Grade 4

Sometimes it is really windy and cold, very cold and very choppy waves on the sea. We were on our way to Shawn Nutuk's outpost camp but the wind was so strong that it blew Joilie's cap away. We returned to camp as the water was too rough and once we were there, we set up the tent. We waited for the storm to calm down and began our return to Arctic Bay. The sea was less choppy then.

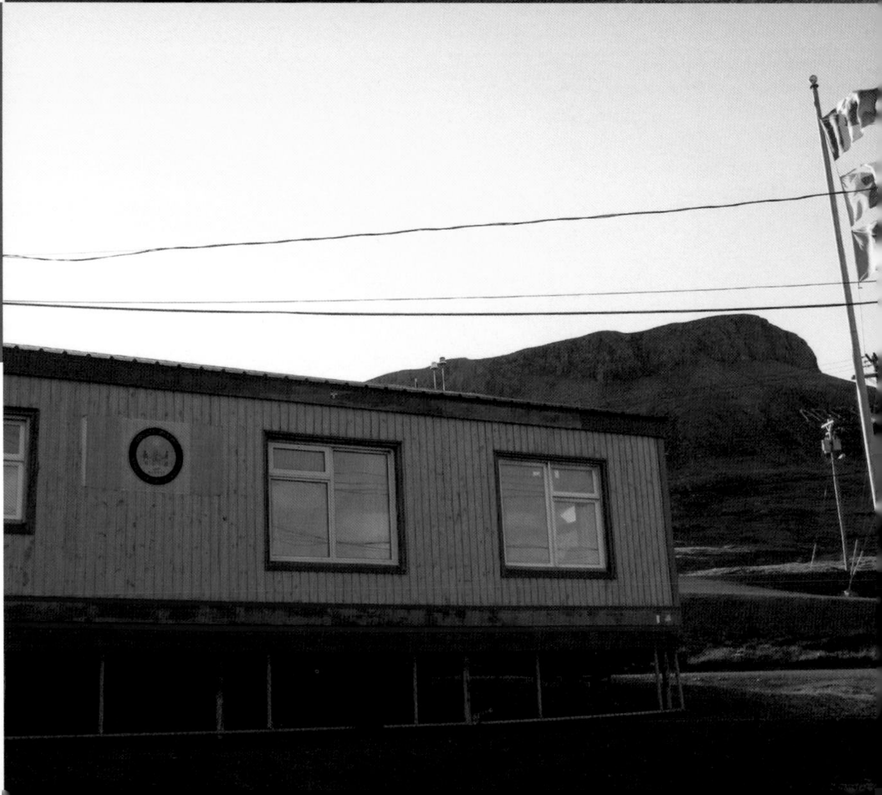

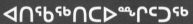

ᐊᑎᖅᖃᖅᑎᑕᐅᖏᓐᕋᑐᖅ

ᐋᓐᔭᓚ ᑕᖅᑐ, ᐊᕐᒡᒍᓚᓂᒃ 9, ᒍᓈᓗ 4

ᐊᐅᓪᓚᕐᔪᑎᓐᑦ ᐃᒡᓚᖅᐋᕐᔪᑎᓐᑦ ᐃᓗᐃᑦᑐᒥᒃ ᐊᐅᓪᓚᕐᔪᑎᓐᑦ ᓴᓂᖕᓂᒃ ᖅᐱᒃᔮᔪᑎᓐᑦ ᐃᒡᓚᐃᐱᑎᐳᑉ ᐊᐅᒃᒐᔮᖕᒍ ᖅᐱᓕᓗᓅᑦ ᑎᖕᒦᐋᒍᒻᑦ ᓂᕆᓂᑲᔅᑐᒻᑦ ᓂᑎᖕᐹᕐᐋᖁᓚᓱ ᔅᑕᔭᐊᒥᒃ ᐊᒃᑎᓕᓂᓚ ᐋᖅᓴᖁᖅᔪᓚᔪᑐᐅᖃ ᐊᒃᓚᖅᖃᑎᕐᓕᒻᑦ ᐊᒃᔅᔭᖅᖃᑲᓪ ᖯᒃᐋᓯᕐ ᐊᑎᐱᑦᑐᔭᔭᖅᑐᕐᓕᓚ ᐊᓗᒌᔷᕐᔪᒍᔭᖅᑐᓚ ᑎᖕᒦᐋᒍᒻ ᔅᑯᒃᓅᖅᔮᖃᓚᖅᔭᔭᑐᖅ ᐊᒻᐃᓗ ᖴᕐᒡᒻ ᐃᒥᐋᒐᐋᖅᖃᑦᖁᓗᕐᑦ ᐊᒻᐃᓚ ᖅᐋᐋᕐᖃᓂᓗᕐᑦ ᐅᑦᕐᔪᐃᑦ.

Untitled

Angela Taqtu, Age 9, Grade 4

Once you buy a whole can of soda while traveling, and leave the plastic wrap around the soda can, a bird trying to get something to eat would come across the plastic and get it stuck on its beak as it has no hands. The bird would not be able to remove the plastic, but only by cutting the plastic would this not happen and also, throw your garbage carefully away or cover them with rocks.

It's a great summer day, my father is taking me for a walk. I can hear birds, smell the grass and feel the hot sun.

Untitled
Chad McGraw, Age 6

It's a great summer day, my father is taking me for a walk. I can hear birds, smell the grass and feel the hot sun.

ᐊᑎᖅᖃᖅᑎᑕᐅᖏᑦᑐᖅ
ᓴᑦ ᒪᒍᕋᐤ, 06-ᓂ�b ᐅᑭᐅᑕ�b

ᐅᑦᑐᖅ ᐊᐅᔭᖅᑎᐊᕿᐅᑦᑐᓂ
ᐱᐸᑦᑎᐊᖅᑐᖅ, ᐊᑖᑕᓗ ᐱᓕᖃᐅᓄ�b.
ᑎᖑᒐᓂb ᑐᓯᔪᕐᐊᖅᑐᔎ, ᓇᐃᒪᐅᓗᑕᓗ
ᐃᕕᖏᓂb ᐊᓗᓗ ᓯᖁᓂᐅᐸ ᐅᖅᑯᓐᓇᓗ
ᐃbᐱᓕᒍᕐᐊᓐᓄᓗᒍ.

ᖃᕆᓂb ᐊᐃᐱᓕᑕ, 09-ᓂb ᐅᑭᐅᑕb, ᒍᓂᓚ 4
Veronica Ipeelee, Age 10, Grade 4

ᔪ ᐊᑕᒍᑦᕝᐊᖅ, 09-ᓂb ᐅᑭᐅᑕb, ᒍᓂᓚ 4
Joe Attagutsiak, Age 9, Grade 4

peelee

Joe Attag...
Age: 9 ...
Arctic Ba...

ᐊᕐᕕᐊᑦ	Arviat
ᑎᑭᕋᕐᔪᐊᖅ	Whale Cove
ᑲᖏᖅᖠᓂᖅ	Rankin Inlet
ᑭᙵᐅᑦ	Cape Dorset
ᐃᖃᓗᐃᑦ	Iqaluit
ᐸᖕᓂᖅᑐ	Pangnirtung
ᒥᑦᑎᒪᑕᓕᒃ	Pond Inlet
ᒥᑦᑎᒪᑕᓕᒃ	Nanisivik
ᐃᒃᐱᐊᕐᔪᒃ	Arctic Bay
ᖃᐅᓱᐃᑦᑐᖅ	Resolute Bay
ᐊᐅᓱᐃᑦᑐᖅ	Grise Fiord

ᖃᐅᓯᐊᑦᑐᖅ
ᖃᖅᒪᖅᑕᓕᒃ ᐃᓕᓐᓂᐊᕆᕕᒃ

ᖃᐅᓯᐊᑦᑐᖅ ᐃᓄᒃᐊᖑᖅ ᕼᐋᒪᓚᐅᖅ 250-ᓂᒃ ᐃᓄᒃᐃᖅᑎᓕᒃᓂ ᑐᐸᒃᐊᑰᒃᖏᓕᒃᓄ ᑲᓇᑕᒥ ᓄᓇᓕᕇᕈᓴᓂ. ᐊᖅᑎᕐᒐᓕᕐᕈᓂᒃ ᐃᓄᕐᓄ ᐊᖅᖃᓂᕐᑎᕐᑕᐅᒃᓄ ᕘᖏᓂᒃᓄ, ᐊᒻᓗ ᔪᕐᕐᕙᑕᓕᒃ ᓴᓇᑐᐃᕐᓂᒃ ᖃᐅᐱᓂᕐᑎᓂᒃ ᓯᓕᕐᕐᐊᕆᕇᑕᐅᒃᓄ ᓄᓇᕐᖁᐊᑯ ᑲᕐᕐᓕᒃᓄ ᖃᐅᐱᓂᕐᒐᐅᒃᑕᕐᕐᓄᓂ. ᐊᐅᕐᐊᑕᖅ ᐅᕐᖃᕐᑲᐅᖅᑐᖃ ᐊᒻᓗ ᖁᕐᒍᖃᖅᑐᓄ ᐊᒻ ᑕᕐᕇᓇᖅ. ᐃᓄᒃᑎᑐᒃ ᖃᐅᓯᐊᑦᑐᖅ ᖁᑦᐊᒍᖅᐋᓇᕇᒃᓂ. ᑕᐱᒃᓄ ᐅᑭᐅᖅᑕᖅᑐᒃ ᑭᓕᓇᒍᐊᖅᓕᑕ ᑦᖅᒃᑕᓂᕐᖃ ᐊᓕᕐᑎᓂᕐᓄᒍ. ᑕᐋᒻᐊᓇᒃᑕᐅᒃᑕ, ᖃᐅᓯᐊᑦᑐᖅ ᐊᐅᕐᐊᑕᕇᖅᖃᓕᒃ ᐃᒃᕐᓇᕐᕆ 24-ᓂᒃ ᓯᖅᑲᐅᒍᐊᖅᑲᒃᑐᖅ. ᓄᓇᓕᐊᕆᖅ ᐊᕈᑎᒃᑕᖅ ᐸᓂᖅᑐᓇᓗ, ᓯᑎᓗᒃᐊᒃᑕᕇᓇᒍ.

Resolute Bay
Qarmartalik School

Resolute is a small hamlet of 250, and is the second most northerly community in Canada. It is known as the home of some of the greatest Inuit hunters, and is also the starting point for many international scientific research teams to the North Pole. Resolute is filled with rocky coastal bluffs and gravel flats, as well as deposits of glacial moraine and some small lakes. Resolute is known as Qausuittuq in Inuktitut, which means "place with no dawn," because of the long winter nights. By the same token, Resolute experiences twenty-four-hour sunshine during the summers. The community is very windy and arid, with a general lack of precipitation.

ᔐᐃᒥ
Jamie

JAMIE

D.N. SALLUVINIQ
ᑖᓂᐊᕝ ᕼᐳᕕᓂᖅ

ᐊᕐᕕᐊᑦ	Arviat
ᑎᑭᕋᕐᔪᐊᖅ	Whale Cove
ᑲᖏᖅᖠᓂᖅ	Rankin Inlet
ᑭᙵᐃᑦ	Cape Dorset
ᐃᖃᓗᐃᑦ	Iqaluit
ᐸᖕᓂᖅᑑ	Pangnirtung
ᒥᑦᑎᒪᑕᓕᒃ	Pond Inlet
ᓇᓂᓯᕕᒃ	Nanisivik
ᐃᒃᐱᐊᕐᔪᒃ	Arctic Bay
ᖃᐅᓱᐃᑦᑐᖅ	Resolute Bay
ᐊᐅᔪᐃᑦᑐᖅ	Grise Fiord

⊲⊳ᒧ⊿ᐊᑦᑐᖅᑿ
⊳ᒥᒡᒪᖷ ⊿ᑕᐤᓂᐊᖅᕕᖷ

Grise Fiord
Umimmak School

⊲⊳ᒧ⊿ᐊᑦᑐᖅᑿ ⊿ᓄᖅᑯᐊᒻᑎᑐᐤᓗ ᓄᐊᓕᐤ ⊳ᑭⅅᖅᑕᒥ ⊳ᖳᒪᓂᖅᑿ‹⊲᷒ᖅ ᑐᓄᐊᐊᔪᐣᗔᓗ ᑲᓇᑕᒥ. ᐃᖁᐳᑦ ⊲ᑕᓂ ⊲ᒡᒪᗔ ᑲᖾᑎᑐᖷᒥ, ⊿ᓄᖅᖅᑿ 150-ᓂ ⊲ᒥᒃᑎᑎᖅᗔ. ⊲ᔮᗔᐳᗦᒪᓂᗔᒡᗞ ᑭᖷᒃᔭᐊ, ⊲⊳ᒧ⊿ᐊᑐᖅᑿ ᄾᖅᔮ᷒ᐊᔮⅅᑐᖅᑿ. ⊲⊳ᐦᒥ, ⊳ᑕᗦᗔᑕᖅᑿ ⊿ᑭᖅ᷒ᓂ 24--ᓂ ᔾᖅᓂᓂᔾᖅᑐᖅᑿ, ᑭᔮᓂᑕ ᑕ⊿ᒪⅅᑲᗦ⊲᷒ᖅᑎᑐᒧ ᓄᐊᖷ ⊲ᐳᗔᐊᑭᕮ᷒ᖅᑎᑐᖅᑿ ᗦᑯᐊᒻᒪᐤᐊᗞᗔᓗᒧ. ᑕⅉᑲᓂ ⊳ᑭⅅᖅᑕᖅᑐᗦ ᑭᗦᓂᒻᒨⅎᐊᖷ᷒ᒪᑕ ᑲᓇᖁᓂᓗᓂ 1,160-ᓂᗞ ᑭⅉᒪᑕᓂᗞ ᖅᑲᓂᓂᖅᗞᓂᗞᒡᗞ, ⊲⊳ᒧ⊿ᐊᑦᑿ ⊿ᔾᗔⅉᔾᖅᑿ, ⊲ᒡᒪᗔ ⊿ᑭᐤ᷒ᗔᓂᖅᗔᐁ᷒ᒪᖅᑐᓂ ⊿ᒪᐤᐊⅡᒥ -50°C.

The sparsely populated hamlet of Grise Fiord is the northernmost community in Canada. Situated under sheer cliffs and at the top of a scenic fiord, it has a population of about 150. It is protected by the mountains of the Arctic Cordillera range, and as a result Grise Fiord does not have harsh winds. During the summer months, it has twenty-four-hour sunshine, but even in those months the community never totally thaws. Located 1,160 kilometres north of the Arctic Circle, Grise Fiord is very cold, and extreme midwinter temperatures can be as low as –50°C.

ᖁᓄᖅ ᓯᓚᐅᑉ ᐊᔾᔨᒌᑎᑕᐅᓂᖕᒪ ᐊᕙᑎᑦᑎᓂᖅ

ᕋᓯᓪ ᐊᑯᓚᒍᖅ

ᓯᓚ ᐊᔾᔨᒌᑐᑕᐅᑦᑐᖅ ᐊᕙᑎᑦᑎᓂᖅ ᐱᒍᒃᖑᒪᒥᒃ ᓄᓇᒥ ᐊᐅᓪᓚᖅᓯᒪᑎᓪᓗᒋ, ᐱᓱᒡᒍᖏᓂᖅᒃᔪᐊᒋᓗᓂ ᓄᓇᓕᖕᒥᓂ.

ᓄᓇᒥ ᐊᐅᓪᓚᖅᓯᒪᓗᓂ ᓯᓴᓐᖔᐊᕐᖁᑐ ᑐᒪᓕᕐᑕᕐᑭᒡ ᒪᓐᒃᔪᓂ ᓯᓚᐅᑉ ᖁᓄᐊᒥᓂᖕᓂᒃ. ᓯᓚ ᐱᐅᑦᑎᓐᑦᓗᒍ ᑕᖕᒪᖅᑖᖑᓪᒥ ᓇᑎᐊᖅᖃᖑᑦᑐᖅ ᐅᑕᖅᑭᓂ ᓯᓚᐅᑉ ᐱᐅᓯᓂᐅᔪᖕᓂᒃᒃ. ᖁᓄᖅᑐ ᖅᖁᐊᕐᔫᖕᓂᒃᖄᐅᐸᐅᑦ ᖅᐹᑎᐊᓐᔪᖕᐁᑦ ᓯᓚ ᐱᑕᓐᒍ, ᐊᔾᔾᖓᐊᖕᑐᖅ. ᐊᔾᔾᑕᓐᖕᖕᖅ ᐅᑕᖅᒃᕆᒡᓗᓂ ᑭᓯᐊᓂ.

ᐊᒥᒍ ᐃᓄᐃᑦ ᓯᖅᐱᓐᖓᓐᖃᑦᐁᓂᓚᕐᖅᖄᑕ, ᐊᒥᒍ ᐃᑕᕌᑦ ᐊᒃᑐᖅᑕᐅᓂᖅᖄᕐᖅᐅᑦ ᐊᖐᒥᑦ ᐊᓂᖅᑐᖅ ᐊᖕᓗ ᐊᔾᖕᓂᖅᒃ ᐱᔾᓐᖔᖕᖅᐅᑦ.

ᐊᒃᑕᐅᖅ ᓇᓚᐅᑎᒋᔪᐊᓐᖔᒡ ᓯᒡᒥ ᒪᓚᕆᓐᒡᑐ ᖃᑎᐅᓂᖅ ᑕᕐᖕᖓᓗᔭᐅᕐᖅ ᓴᖃᐁᒡᒪᐁᓪ ᐊᐅᑦᑎᖅᓯᒪᑐᒡᑐ ᒪᓐᖃᐊᑦᑐᒍ ᖃᕕᐅᓴᐁᖅᖕᖃ ᐱᖅᒃᖕᖅᓐᐸᖅᒡᑦ, ᐃᑕᑐᖅᐴᖅᖄᖕᖅᓂᒍ, ᓇᓪᖕᖓᒻᒡᔫᖕᖔᐁ ᖃᕕᐅᑕᖕᐊᒃᖃᖕᖔᕕᕐᓚᕐᖏᑦ.

ᓯᓚ ᐊᖅᑐᐊᑐᐃᐊᖕᖏᕐᑦᖄ ᐊᖕᓇᖃᐊᒡᑐᖅᖃᓐᖕᓐᑦᓂᖕᒃ ᖄᓇᕐᖅ ᓴᖃᓐᖕᐊᑕᐃᖅᐅᑦᖃ ᓐᖓᓐᒃ. ᐊᔾᓐᖓᐁᑦ ᖅᖃᔾᖅᖕᐧᖕᐁᑐᖅᖕᓂ ᐅᒃ ᑭᒃᖕᖓᒃ ᐊᖕᖕᖃ ᖅᕕᓐᖕᖔᓂᖕᒃ, ᐅᐁᖕᖕᒥᒡᒡᒡ ᑭᕕᓐᐊ ᓯᓪᒥ ᐸᖕᓂᖕᔾᓐᖔᑦᖄᒡᑐ ᓯᖅᖕᓯᓐᒡᑦᖄᕐ ᐊᒡᒥᖅ ᓯᖅᒃᖃᑕᐅᖃᒍ.

ᓯᓚ ᐊᖅᑐᐃᓯᕐᒡᖄ ᐊᕐᖓᓐᖕᒃ ᑲᒪᖃᓐᖕᖓᒍ ᐅᓚᖕᓂᓐᐊᑐᖅ ᑲᒪᖕᓐᖕᖓᖔᖕᖄᑦ ᒡᑐᖄᒡᑦᖄ ᐅᖕᒥᒪᓐᐊ ᐴᖔᕐᖅᖔ ᓯᓚᓐᖕᖄᖅᖕᐸᕐᖄ ᖅᐊᖕᖔᐸᐧᖄᑕᒡᕐᖕᐊᖅᖄᒡ ᖅᐨᐊᖕᖕᖔᖕᐧᓐᐧᐁᑐᖄᑐ ᓯᔥᓐᖕ ᖅᖕᓇᖕᖄᒃ ᖃᖕᐊᔾᓐᒡᕐᑐᐊᖔᖕᐧᒍ. ᐴᖅᒥᖕᓐᓗᖃᑐᖅ ᖃᕕᐅᒍᖕᓐᓚᖕᒍᕐᖄᒡ, ᑕᐃᖃᐊ ᐴᕐᔾᐊᑦ ᓂᓇᖁᖕᖃᕐᖔᒡ.

How Weather Affects Your Environment

Russell Akulagok

The weather affects our environment a lot when we are out on the land, but not so much in the community.

Out on the land what you do is what is determined by what the weather is like. If the weather is bad then you have to stay at camp until it gets better. No matter how much you say or cry about the weather, it won't change. It will change when it wants to.

Most people want it to be sunny all the time, but it would affect lots of animals who rely on the snow and other things.

It's nice to be able to predict the weather without the help of a radio or TV because when you are out hunting and you know there is a blizzard coming, you need to be in a place where there is snow to build an iglu, or in a sheltered place.

The weather does not affect only humans. It also affects the animals, like seals. In April, seals have to give birth to pups. In order to do that they need snow to keep warm. During the spring baby seals never go on the ice when the sun is out and there is no wind. When there is no sun and there is wind the big seals hardly go on the ice.

The weather also affects our traditional clothing when they are made. When the women bleach the skins of a seal for women's kamiks, they do this in April because the sun is not too hot to burn the leather.

The weather affects the environments for animals like caribou or muskoxen. If it was raining before the ground froze, it would be hard for the caribou and muskoxen to eat because the top part of the ground would be ice. This would affect us, too, because we eat the animals.

ᐊᖓᑦᑯᖅ ᐊᐅᓚᑦᓯᓇᓂᖅᑎᑦᑐᒍ ᓯᓚᒥᒃ

ᐋᓐᑐᕉ ᓄᙵᖅ

ᑐᓴᐅᒪᔪᖓ ᐊᒻᒪᓗ ᐅᖃᓪᒫᖅᓯᒪᑦᑐᖓ ᐅᓂᒃᑲᐅᓯᕐᓂᒃ ᓯᓚᒥᒃ ᐱᔾᔪᑎᖃᖅᑐᓂᒃ. ᐊᑕᐅᓯᖅ ᐅᓂᒃᑳᕐᔪᐊᖅ ᐊᖓᑦᑯᕈᖅ ᐊᐅᓚᑦᓯᔪᓇᖅᑐᖅ ᓯᓚᒥᒃ. ᐊᖓᑦᑯᐃᑦ ᐱᐅᙱᑦᑑᔪᓇᕐᒪᑕ ᐃᓄᖕᓄᑦᑐ ᐱᑦᑎᐊᙱᔪᓇᖅᑐᑎᒃ. ᐊᖓᑦᑯᖅ ᓯᓚᒥᒃ ᐊᓄᓈᓂᖅᑎᑦᑎᔪᓇᖅᑐᖅ ᐅᕝᕙᓘᓐᓃ ᓄᖅᑲᖅᑎᑦᑎᔪᓇᖅᑐᓂ. ᑕᐃᒪᓕ ᐊᖓᑦᑯᖅ ᐱᐅᙱᑦᑐᖅ ᐱᖅᓯᖅᑎᑦᑎᔪᓇᖅᑐᖅ ᐊᖑᓇᓱᓪᓗᓂ ᐊᔪᕐᓇᖅᑎᑦᑎᓗᓂ. ᐅᖃᓪᒫᖅᓯᒪᔪᖓ ᐅᖃᓪᒥ ᐊᖑᒻᒥᒃ ᖃᐅᔨᒪᓂᖅᑐᒥᒃ ᐊᖓᑦᑯᒥᒃ, ᐊᒻᒪᓗ ᐅᖃᖅᓯᒪᑦᑐᓂ ᐋᓂᐊᖅᑐᓂᒃ ᐊᖅᑭᒃᓱᕐᓇᕐᓂᖏᓐᓂᒃ ᐊᒻᒪᓗ ᓯᕗᓂᕐᒥᒃ ᖃᐅᔨᒪᔪᓇᖅᑐᓂᒃ. ᐊᑕᐅᓯᖅ ᐅᓂᒃᑲᐅᓯᖅ ᐅᖃᖅᓯᒪᔪᖅ ᐊᖓᑦᑯᕈᖅ ᐱᐅᙱᑦᑐᖅ ᐳᐊᕐᓇᓴᕐᓂᕐᒪᑦ ᓄᕗᔭᒥ ᐳᑐᓯᑦᑐᓂ, ᖄᖓᓃᑦᑐᓂ ᓄᕗᔭᐳ, ᐃᓄᐃᑦ ᑳᓕᕐᑯᑦᑐᑎᑦ. ᐃᑲᔪᖅᑕᐅᔪᒪᓂᕐᒧᑦ ᕿᓄᓂᕐᒪᑕ. ᐊᖓᑦᑯᒧᑦ ᐊᓯᐊᓄᑦ ᐃᑲᔪᖅᑕᐅᓂᕐᒥᒃ ᖁᓪᓗᑦ ᑎᖕᒋᑦᑐᓂ ᐊᐳᒻᒥᒃ ᓯᒥᓐᓂᖅᓱᓂᐅᒃ ᓄᕗᔭ ᐱᖅᑐᖅᑯᓇᒍ. ᑕᐃᒪᓕ ᑖᓐᓇ ᐊᖓᑦᑯᖅ ᐱᐅᙱᑦᑐᖅ ᑕᑯᓐᓂᖅᓱᓂᐅᒃ ᓇᒧᑦ ᐱᖕᒪᖕᒫᑦ ᐊᐅᓪᓚᖅᑐᒃᓴᐅᔪᖅ.

ᐅᓂᒃᑳᑉ ᐊᐃᑉᐸᖓ ᐃᓄᖕᓄᑦ ᖃᐅᔨᒪᔭᐅᔪᖅ ᑕᐃᓐᓇᒎᖅ ᐊᖓᑦᑯᖅ ᐊᑎᓕᒃ ᓴᐅᓗᒥᒃ, ᐱᖅᑐᒥᒃ ᑐᖁᑦᑎᔪᓇᖅᑐᖅ ᐱᖅᑐᐊᓘᓪᓗᐊᖅᑎᑦᑐᒍ. ᑐᐱᐅᑉ ᐃᓗᐊᓄᑦ ᐃᓯᖅᓱᓂ ᐊᖕᒪᐃᑦᑐᓂ ᐊᒡᒐᒥᑐᑦ ᑕᐃᒪᓐᓇ ᐊᖏᑎᒋᔭᒥᒃ. ᑎᒍᒥᐊᖅᓱᓂ ᓴᕕᖕᒥᒃ, ᐊᒡᒐᓂ ᓄᐃᑕᑎᑦᑐᓂᐅᒃ, ᐊᒻᒪᓗ ᑐᖁᑦᑎᑦᑐᓂ ᐊᓄᓕᒥᒃ. ᑕᒪᐃᑦᑐᕕᓂᖅ ᐃᓄᐃᓪᓘᖅ ᐊᖑᓇᓱᒍᓇᐃᑦᑕᑦᑐᑎᒃ ᓂᕿᒃᓴᒥᒃ ᐱᔭᓇᐃᑦᑕᓂᕐᒪᑕ. ᐊᒡᒐᓂ ᓯᓚᒧᑦ ᐊᓂᑎᓯᒪᓚᐅᖅᑐᓂᐅᒃ, ᐊᐅᖕᒥᒃ ᑕᑯᒃᓴᐅᔭᖅᑲᖅᑐᕕᓂᖅ ᐊᒡᒐᖓ ᓯᓚᒧᑦ ᓄᐃᑕᑎᑦᑐᒍ.

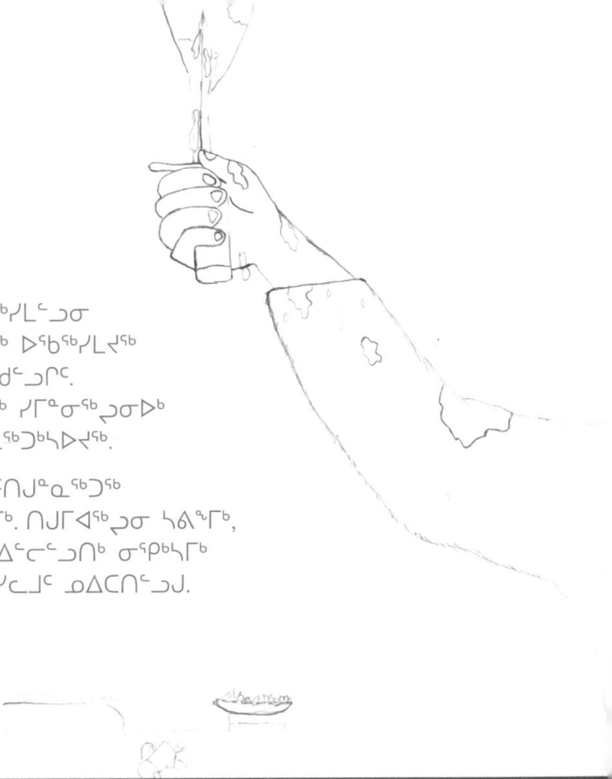

Shaman Controlling the Weather

Andrew Nungaq

I have heard and read some stories that involved the weather. One of them is about a shaman that can control the weather. They can be evil or bad to people. The shaman can make strong winds die down or just make no wind at all. Also the evil shaman can make it snow so much that you will not be able to hunt for food. I have read a book about a guy who has known a shaman, and he said they have power to heal, and also to predict the future. One of the stories about a shaman was when an evil shaman shoveled a hole in one of the clouds, while on top of the cloud, so the people would be starved. They had called out for help. It was another shaman and he saved the people when he flew up to the cloud and plugged the hole to stop it from snowing. This is when he saw the shaman on top and I guess he had gone away.

Another story that people heard was about a shaman named Saullu, who could kill the wind even if it was the worst storm ever. He would go inside a tent and make a hole large enough to fit his hand through. He would hold a knife, strike his hand out, and kill the wind. The reason why he had done this is because the people couldn't go out and hunt for food. After he had struck his hand out, there was blood running down while his hand was up.

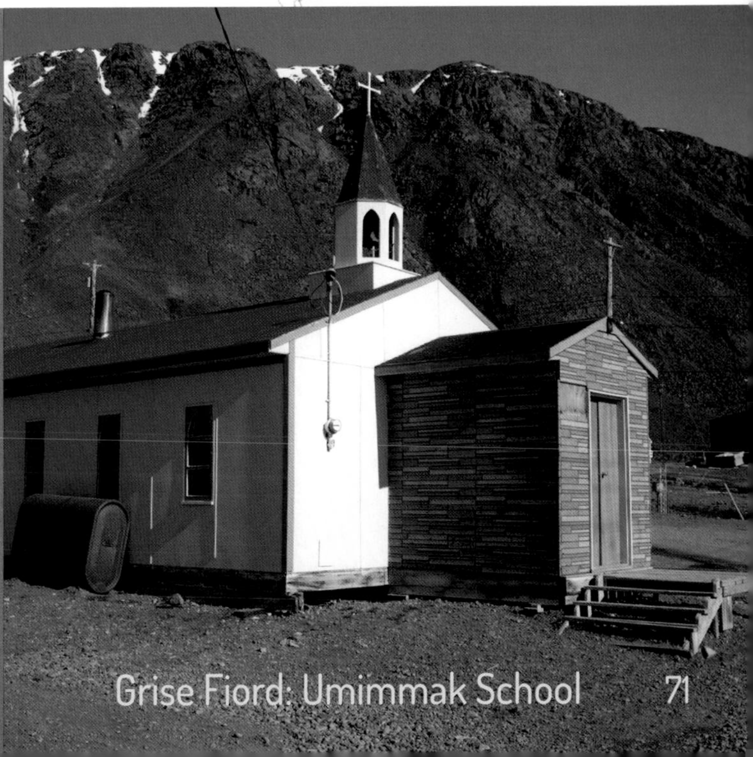

ᐅᑭᐅᑦ ᐅᖅᑯᒐᖅᓂᖅᓴᐅᓯᐊᑦ, ᐊᐳᑎᖅᑲᖃᕐᓂᖅᓴᐅᓯᐊ ... ᖃᓄᐃᓕᐅᕝᔫᖅᐳ ᓯᓚ ᐊᓯᔾᔨᖅᐸᑕ

ᒋᐊᑦ ᐊᑕᒍᑦᓯᐊᖅ

ᐅᑭᐅᑦ ᐅᖅᑯᒐᖅᓂᖅᓴᐅᓯᐊᑦ
ᐊᐳᑎᖅᑲᖃᕐᓂᖅᓴᐅᓯᐊᑦ
ᖃᓄᐃᓕᐅᕝᔫᖅᐳ ᓯᓚ ᐊᓯᔾᔨᖅᐸᑦᑕ?
ᐃᓕᖅᑯᓯᕐᑐᖅᓴᐅᐃ ᐊᒃᑐᖅᑕᐅᓕᕈᖕᓂᖅ

ᓯᓚᐅᑉ ᖃᓄᐃᓐᓂᓕ ᐊᖏᒐᓯ
ᓯᓚᐅᑉ ᖃᓄᐃᓐᓂᓕ ᐊᖏᒐᓐᓂᐸᑦᑕ
ᖃᓄᓂᑦ ᐃᐅᐱᓇᓴᖅᐸᑦ ᓯᓚᐃᑦ ᖃᓄᐃᓐᓂᓕ ᐊᓯᔾᔨᖅᐸᑕ?
ᐊᓯᔾᔨᑎᓂᐅᑉᐸᓯᖕᒋᑎᑎᖃᐃ

ᐅᑭᐅᑦ ᐅᖅᑯᒐᖅᓂᖅᓴᐅᓯᐊᑦ
ᐊᐳᑎᖅᑲᖃᕐᓂᖅᓴᐅᓯᐊᑦ
ᖃᓄᐃᓕᐅᕝᔫᖅᐳ ᓯᓚ ᐊᓯᔾᔨᖅᐸᑕ?
ᐊᓯᔾᔨᖅᓂᖅᑲᐃ ᐊᒻᒪᕐᒪᑎᓐᓇᐊᖅᖃᖅᑕᐊᑦ.

Warmer Winters, More Snow... What Would Happen If Your Climate Changed

Gail Attagutsiak

Warmer winters
More snow
What would happen if your climate changed?
Maybe it would change our cultural ways

The climate is mine
And the climate is yours
How would you feel if the climate has changed?
Maybe you'd become a way of change

Warmer winters
More snow
What would happen if the climate changed?
Maybe you'd have to accept the change.

Grise Fiord: Umimmak School   73

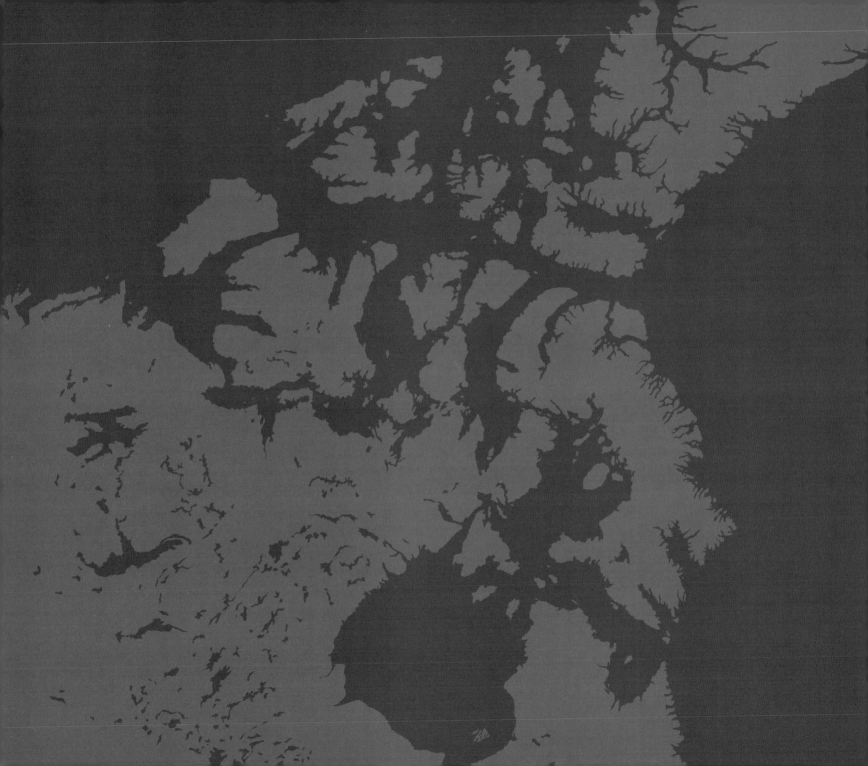

ᖅᑯᔪᖕᓇᒦᖅᑕᐅᔪᑦ ᐃᕚᓐ ᐱᓚᓐ-ᐅᐊᓚᔅ,
ᑕᐃᕕᔅ ᕼᐅᑐᑦ, ᐊᒻᓗ ᐃᓄᖕᓂᐊᖅᑎᓯᔪᑕᑦ
ᐃᓄᖕᓂᐊᖅᑎᓪᓗ ᐃᓚᒋᔭᐅᓚᐅᖅᑐᑦ
ᐅᑭᐅᖅᑕᖅᑐᒥ ᓯᓚᓕᕆᓂᕐᒧᑦ
ᓴᓇᒃᓴᑎᐅᓚᐅᖅᑐᒧᑦ 1994-ᒥ

Thank you to Yvonne Bilan-Wallace, Davis
Whittle, and the teachers and students who
participated in the original Arctic Weather
Centre contest in 1994.